Copyright

The Ultimate Horror Collection
By
Tina Wingham

Contents

Warning

This novel contains themes and scenes intended to evoke fear and suspense, including depictions of psychological distress, supernatural elements, violence, and moments of intense emotional tension.

Some readers may find certain content unsettling or disturbing. Reader discretion is advised.

If you are sensitive to themes involving trauma, death, or intense fear, please take care while reading.

The Reckoning Of Jason

Prologue

The afternoon sun hung lazily in the sky, casting warm golden light over the rippling waters of the stream. Lush green foliage lined the banks, the scent of damp earth and wildflowers drifting through the air. Laughter echoed through the valley as Jason splashed water toward his wife and daughter, their carefree giggles blending with the chirping of birds overhead.

"Daddy, no fair!" Lily shrieked with delight, dodging the playful spray as she kicked her tiny feet against the cool water. Her golden hair glistened in the sunlight, sticking to her cheeks as she tried to splash him back.

Jason chuckled, shaking droplets from his arms. "Oh, you think you can take me, huh?"

His wife, Emily, waded up beside them, her smile as radiant as the sun reflecting off the water. "Be careful, sweetheart. Your father doesn't know how to lose."

Jason gasped in mock offence. "I'll have you know I'm an excellent loser!" He paused, then smirked. "I just never lose."

Lily erupted into another fit of giggles as Emily rolled her eyes and sent a small wave of water toward him, earning a playful yelp in response. They stayed there, enjoying the warmth of the day, time slowing to a peaceful hum, as if the world beyond the valley didn't exist.

But it did.

As the sun dipped lower, the crisp air of evening settled over them. Jason scooped Lily into his arms, pressing a kiss to her damp forehead before setting her down on the grassy bank. "Alright, little fish, time to dry off."

Lily pouted but obeyed, wrapping herself in a towel as Emily gathered their belongings. Jason took a deep breath, savouring the moment.

Tomorrow, they would return to the city. Back to normal life.

The sterile, fluorescent-lit hallways of the lab awaited him—a stark contrast to the wild beauty of the stream. But he didn't mind. He liked his job. It was quiet, predictable, and allowed him to come home every evening to the two people he loved most in the world.

Jason took one last look at the sunlit valley before turning toward the path leading home. He had everything he ever wanted.

And for now, that was enough.

Chapter 1

The rain fell in sheets against the city, turning the streets into reflective pools of neon and shadow. The gutters overflowed, carrying away cigarette butts, scraps of discarded paper, and the filth of a city that never truly slept. A siren wailed in the distance, merging with the hum of traffic and the occasional honk of a frustrated driver. In the heart of this restless metropolis, Jason moved like a ghost, slipping between alleyways and side streets, unseen and unnoticed. He preferred it that way.

Jason's apartment sat above an abandoned laundromat, its once-bright sign now a faded relic of better days. The windows were boarded up, though the boards themselves had begun to rot. The building sagged under the weight of neglect, much like its lone occupant. Inside, the air smelled of dust, gun oil, and the faint remnants of whiskey. The furniture was sparse—a single battered couch, a rickety wooden table covered in scattered ammunition and a half-eaten meal, and a mattress on the floor. The walls were bare, save for a single photograph taped above the bed.

A little girl with golden hair and a bright, toothy smile.

Jason sat at the table, the bottle of whiskey beside him was nearly empty, its amber contents reduced to the final swallows. He hadn't touched it in hours. Drinking dulled the edge, and Jason didn't want the edge dulled— not anymore. He needed to feel the weight of it, the sharp press of reality against his ribs. It reminded him that he was still breathing, even when he wished he wasn't.

Lily had been six when she died.

And he had never forgiven himself.

The hospital had smelled sterile, too clean, too artificial. Machines beeped, doctors whispered, and nurses bustled about with the efficiency of people who had seen death too many times to

17

flinch at its approach. Jason had held her tiny hand, his rough fingers dwarfing hers, whispering stories of faraway places. She had loved those stories—tales of knights and explorers, of deep-sea adventures and journeys to the stars. Her eyelids had fluttered, her breathing shallow, and in that final moment, she had smiled at him.

Then she was gone.

Emily had been beside him, her sobs muffled against his shoulder. He had held her for a long time, his own grief lodged so deep in his chest that he couldn't make a sound. That night, he had promised her they would survive this together. That they would grieve, heal, and somehow, find a way forward.

But Jason had lied.

The house had grown colder after Lily's death. Like something had drained all the warmth from its walls, leaving only shadows and silence behind. Jason had withdrawn, barricading himself behind a wall of numbness that Emily could not breach.

"Talk to me, Jason," she had pleaded one night, her voice trembling with frustration and sorrow. "Please. We need to get through this together."

Jason had stared at her from the couch, his eyes vacant. "There's nothing to talk about."

"Nothing to—" Her voice cracked, and she let out a bitter laugh, shaking her head. "Lily is gone. Our daughter is dead, and you act like— like she never existed!"

Jason's jaw clenched. "Don't," he warned.

"Don't what?" she snapped. "Don't talk about her? Don't cry? Don't grieve? Because that's all I've been doing while you sit here and drink yourself into oblivion!"

I'm handling it," he said flatly.

"Handling it?" Emily's eyes burned with fury. "You've shut me out. You won't look at me, won't touch me, won't even say her name." She took a shaky breath, her voice dropping to a whisper. "Jason, I lost her too."

Jason's fingers tightened around the whiskey glass. He couldn't meet her gaze, couldn't face the raw emotion in her eyes. "Then maybe you should go," he murmured.

The silence that followed was deafening.

Emily's breath hitched, as if he had struck her. "What?"

He swallowed hard, staring at the floor. "I don't have anything left to give you, Em."

A strangled sob escaped her lips. "You promised," she whispered. "You promised we'd get through this together."

Jason closed his eyes. He couldn't bear to see her like this—to see the love they had built unraveling in front of him. "I can't," he admitted, his voice hollow. "I don't know how."

Emily wiped at her tears, her hands shaking. "I can't do this alone, Jason. And I won't stand here and watch you destroy yourself."

She turned then, grabbing her coat with trembling fingers. Jason didn't stop her. He didn't move, didn't call out, didn't fight. The door opened, and for a brief moment, he thought she might hesitate.

She didn't.

The door shut behind her with finality, and Jason was alone.

Chapter 2

Jason sat hunched over the bar, the smell of stale beer and sweat thick in the air. The dim pub was filled with the usual types—men drowning regrets, broken souls looking for solace in the bottom of a glass. A jukebox played some old Cold Chisel rock song in the corner, but the lyrics were drowned out by the murmur of voices and the occasional burst of laughter.

He poured another whiskey down his throat, feeling the burn claw its way to his stomach. It did nothing. Just another empty promise of oblivion that never quite delivered. The bartender, a grizzled old man with a belly hanging over his belt, eyed him warily.

"You sure you don't wanna slow down, mate?" he asked, wiping down a glass with a rag that looked dirtier than the counter.

Jason barely acknowledged him. "I'll slow down when I fucking feel like it."

The bartender sighed but didn't argue. Jason could tell the man had seen plenty of lost causes come through here. He wasn't special.

He wasn't different. Just another broken man trying to outdrink his demons.

After what felt like an eternity of drowning in booze, Jason finally peeled himself off the stool and staggered toward the door. The cold night air hit him like a slap, the contrast between the suffocating heat of the bar and the open street sobering him just enough to put one foot in front of the other.

He was halfway home when he heard it.

A dull *thud*, followed by a pained whimper. Then a voice, thick with rage.

"You fucking useless bitch! You ever mouth off to me again, I swear to Christ—" *Another hit.*

Jason stopped dead in his tracks. His pulse slowed. His vision cleared, sharp as a blade. He turned toward the alleyway just off the main road, where the noises were coming from. In the dim orange glow of the streetlamp, he saw them.

A man—big, broad-shouldered, fists clenched—stood over a woman crumpled against the brick wall. Her lip was split, dark bruises blooming on her cheek. She was whimpering, cowering, arms raised in a feeble attempt to protect herself.

Jason rolled his shoulders, cracking his neck. The whiskey haze evaporated. He felt nothing. No rage, no sympathy. Just an opportunity.

"Oi," he called out, his voice cutting through the night. "Why don't you pick on someone who can hit back?"

The man turned, sneering. "Piss off, mate. This ain't your fuckin' business."

Jason stepped forward, his movements eerily calm. "See, that's where you're wrong. You just made it my business."

The man scoffed, taking a step toward him. "The fuck you gonna do about it?"

Jason didn't answer. He just moved.

His fist connected with the man's nose, a sharp *crack* filling the alleyway. Blood spurted instantly, the bastard barely getting a grunt out before Jason followed up with another punch to the ribs. The man gasped, doubling over, but Jason wasn't done.

He grabbed the man's wrist and twisted, forcing him onto his knees. The woman scrambled away, pressing herself against the wall, eyes wide with terror and something else—hope.

Jason tightened his grip. "You like using your hands, yeah?"

The man snarled, trying to yank his arm free. "Fuckin' let go, you psycho—"

Jason snapped the first finger.

The scream that followed was primal, the kind that came from deep inside a man when he realized he was truly, utterly fucked. Jason didn't flinch. He grabbed the next one.

Snap.

The man howled, writhing, but Jason held firm. Another finger. Another sickening *pop*.

"Stop! Fuck! Please—"

Jason leaned in close, his breath hot against the bastard's ear. "You ever lay a hand on her again, I'll come back and take something you can't live without."

The man sobbed, his body convulsing in pain, snot and tears mixing with the blood dripping from his broken fingers. Jason let go, letting him crumple to the ground.

He should have walked away. Should have left him there, beaten, humiliated.

But something in Jason had changed. Or maybe, it had always been there, buried deep.

He reached down and gripped the man's face, forcing his head up. "Look at me."

The man whimpered.

Jason pressed his thumbs against the man's eyelids.

"No," the bastard gasped, panic flaring. "No, no, please—"

Jason pushed.

The eyes gave way with little resistance, wet and sickening as they burst under his fingers. The scream that tore from the man's throat was like music in Jason's ears, but he still felt nothing. No anger, no triumph. Just an empty satisfaction in a job well done.

He let the man collapse in the dirt, rolling onto his side, wailing in horror. The woman was still there, staring at Jason with something unreadable in her gaze. Fear. Gratitude. Maybe both.

He wiped his hands on his jacket and turned away, the echo of the man's screams following him into the night.

Jason had always known he was good at hurting people. But tonight, for the first time, he realized the truth.

He didn't feel a goddamn thing.

A knock at the door snapped him from his thoughts.

He didn't move immediately. Few people knew he lived here. Fewer still would dare to visit uninvited. Slowly, he stood, reaching for the gun that rested on the table. He moved to the door, silent, every muscle in his body coiled like a predator waiting to strike.

Another knock. Three short raps, precise, controlled.

Jason exhaled and unlocked the door.

The man standing on the other side was short, well-dressed in a dark suit that barely showed signs of the rain outside. He held a black briefcase in one hand, his other adjusting a pair of thin glasses. His face was smooth, unreadable. The kind of man who had spent years perfecting the art of being unremarkable.

"Jason," the man said, his voice crisp. "I have a job for you."

Jason stepped aside without a word, allowing the man to enter. He shut the door behind him, locking it once more.

The man placed the briefcase on the table, snapping it open with a practiced flick of his fingers. Inside was a single folder, a thick stack of crisp hundred-dollar bills, and a flash drive. Jason ignored the money. His eyes went straight to the folder.

The man spoke as Jason flipped it open, scanning the contents.

"You don't have to waste your talents on nothing, Jason. Hurting people—hurting the *right* people—pays big. And it's not just about the money. It's about power. Control. You were made for this."

Jason's fingers twitched at the name in the file.

After a long moment, he exhaled.

"I'll take it."

Chapter 3

Jason moved like a shadow through the city, silent, unseen, always watching. He had learned long ago that patience was a hitman's greatest weapon. Killing was easy; it was the preparation, the stalking, the careful unwinding of a man's life that required true skill.

Ted Monroe had no idea he was being followed.

Jason had memorized his routine within the first two days. Ted was predictable, a creature of habit. He left his office at exactly 6:15 p.m., coffee cup in hand, phone to his ear, walking the same route toward the train station. On Tuesdays and Thursdays, he picked up his daughter, Emily, from school. On the weekends, he took her to the park. He wasn't careless—he never lingered in dark places, never took unnecessary detours—but he also wasn't aware.

And that made him easy prey.

Jason followed at a distance, blending into the crowd, always one step behind but never too close. He watched Ted as he laughed with his daughter, as he bought her ice cream and listened to her animated stories. Something twisted in Jason's gut, an echo of a past life, but he pushed it down. This wasn't about sentiment. This was about the job.

Then, something unexpected happened.

Jason had been watching from a nearby bench when a commotion broke out near the entrance of a convenience store. A man—tall, wiry, his clothes hanging loose on his frame—had grabbed a woman's purse and was sprinting toward the street. The woman screamed, stumbling backward, her hands outstretched in disbelief.

Before Jason could even react, Ted was already moving.

Ted Monroe, the man Jason had been hired to kill, took off after the thief without hesitation. His long strides closed the distance quickly, and within moments, he tackled the man to the pavement. There was a struggle, a brief flurry of limbs and grunted curses, but Ted held firm. The thief wriggled, tried to throw a punch, but Ted twisted his arm behind his back and pinned him there, pressing his knee against his spine.

The woman rushed forward, breathless, her face flushed with shock. "Oh my God! Thank you! Thank you so much!"

Ted looked up at her, a little winded but smiling. "You alright?"

She nodded frantically, tears in her eyes. "Yes! Yes, I just—I didn't know what to do. Thank you."

A few passersby had stopped, murmuring in awe at Ted's intervention. The store clerk was already on the phone, calling the police. Ted kept the thief pinned until the wail of sirens approached from down the block. When the officers arrived, they took control, yanking the thief to his feet and stuffing him into the back of the squad car.

Ted dusted himself off, shaking his head with a small chuckle before turning back toward Emily, who stood by the park bench, clutching her stuffed rabbit tightly. "All good, kiddo," he said, ruffling her hair. "Now, how about that ice cream?"

Jason leaned back against the bench, exhaling slowly.

Ted had just finished dropping Emily off at her mother's house. Jason watched from a nearby alley as he walked toward his car, fumbling with his keys. The street was quiet, the hum of distant traffic the only sound.

Jason moved quickly. In three strides, he was behind Ted, wrapping one arm around his throat while pressing a chloroform-soaked cloth against his nose and mouth. Ted struggled, body jerking as his instincts kicked in, but Jason held firm, his grip unbreakable.

Seconds stretched into eternity before Ted's movements slowed, his muscles slackening. Jason lowered him carefully, making sure no one had seen.

He exhaled, checking Ted's pulse. Still alive. Good.

Jason pulled the van door open, lifting Ted inside with practiced ease. The warehouse was waiting.

And soon, Ted Monroe would know what it felt like to be truly powerless.

Chapter 4

Jason had always been meticulous in his work. Surveillance was more than just gathering information—it was about understanding the rhythm of a man's life, dissecting his habits until they became predictable patterns. Ted Monroe would be no different.

Perched in his nondescript black sedan, Jason adjusted the long-lens camera resting in his lap. Across the street, Ted emerged from his apartment complex, a messenger bag slung over his shoulder, the strain in his posture suggesting the weight of more than just files. His suit was well-pressed but slightly loose around the shoulders, a man either losing weight from stress or simply neglecting to take care of himself. Jason took note.

The morning air was thick with humidity, remnants of last night's rain still clinging to the pavement. Pedestrians shuffled past in the early rush, but Jason only had eyes for one man. Ted checked his watch, then walked toward the small café on the corner—a routine Jason had already observed twice before. Predictability was forming.

Jason reached for the worn leather notebook in the passenger seat and flipped it open. The pages were a careful map of Ted's daily movements:

6:45 AM – Leaves apartment
7:00 AM – Café, orders black coffee, toasted bagel
7:30 AM – Arrives at office
12:15 PM – Lunch break, varies between two locations
6:45 PM – Leaves work
7:00 PM – Picks up daughter (Tues/Thurs/Sat)
8:15 PM – Home

Jason had memorised it all, but he wasn't looking for routine—he was looking for vulnerabilities.

That evening, Jason prowled the streets like a panther, his every movement silent, calculated. The city at night belonged to creatures like him—those who watched from the shadows, waiting for the perfect moment to strike. Ted Monroe had no idea how close danger lurked.

A storm had begun rolling in, the air thick with the scent of rain, the oppressive heat of the day giving way to a cool, restless wind. The sky above was a deep, bruised purple, heavy clouds pressing down on the city, rumbling with distant thunder. The occasional flicker of lightning illuminated the wet streets, the reflections of neon signs stretching like liquid fire across the pavement.

Ted exited his office later than usual, his brow furrowed as he scrolled through his phone. Jason followed him from a distance, his footsteps lost in the cacophony of city sounds. Ted turned onto a quieter street, the flickering glow of a broken street lamp casting distorted shadows across the sidewalk.

Then, a scream.

Jason's eyes narrowed as he saw a figure lunging at a woman—a mugger, his movements frantic, desperate. Ted hesitated for only a moment before rushing forward, grabbing the attacker's arm and yanking him back. The woman stumbled away as the mugger twisted, shoving Ted against the alley wall with a grunt.

The rain began to drizzle, turning the pavement slick. The mugger growled, gripping Ted's collar and slamming him against the damp brick wall. "Walk away, old man," he hissed, his breath hot with the stench of stale alcohol. "This ain't your fight."

Ted gritted his teeth, his pulse pounding in his ears. "She was alone," he spat back, forcing his hands between them. "You don't get to pick on people who can't fight back."

The mugger sneered, pressing his forearm against Ted's throat. "And what, you think you're some kinda hero? Look at you, man—you're just a washed-up suit playing knight in shining armor."

Ted struggled, his hands grasping at the mugger's wrist. "Let... go."

"Or what?" The mugger leaned in closer, his grin widening. "Gonna file a complaint? Call the cops? You—"

A sudden burst of strength surged through Ted. He twisted his body, driving his knee into the mugger's gut. The attacker gasped, stumbling backward, his grip loosening just enough for Ted to shove him away.

The mugger cursed, reaching into his jacket. A knife. The blade gleamed as lightning flashed above, reflecting off the wet pavement. Jason tensed in the shadows, his fingers twitching near his sidearm, but he remained still. This was not his fight to interfere with.

Ted squared his shoulders, raising his fists. "You really want to do this?"

The mugger hesitated, eyes darting between Ted's stance and the knife in his own hand. A clap of thunder cracked through the air, reverberating down the alley. The tension held for an excruciating moment before the mugger scoffed, shaking his head. "Ain't worth it."

He turned and disappeared into the night, swallowed by the rain and the darkness.

Ted exhaled, chest heaving. He ran a shaking hand through his damp hair, muttering to himself before turning toward the main road.

Jason remained in the shadows, his expression unreadable. Monroe was not the weak man his file suggested—he was something else entirely. He had instincts, a fire beneath the surface. Jason recognised the kind.

As Ted walked home, shoulders tense, Jason followed, a silent predator in the dark.

Tomorrow, Ted Monroe's life would begin to unravel.

Chapter 5

Ted's consciousness drifted between hazy fragments of memory and the unbearable weight of the present. His head throbbed with a deep, pulsing pain, and the acrid scent of rust and sweat filled his nostrils. His eyelids fluttered open, but the blinding fluorescent light above him forced them shut again.

A chill crawled up his spine. The surface beneath him was cold, unforgiving. Metal. He shifted slightly, only to feel the harsh bite of restraints cutting into his wrists and ankles. Panic surged through him, adrenaline flooding his veins like ice water.

He gasped, straining against the bonds, the sound of his own heavy breathing filling the air. His fingers flexed uselessly, the restraints too tight, too secure. His heart pounded against his ribs as he tried to will away the mounting fear.

A slow, deliberate sound echoed through the room—footsteps. Heavy, methodical, approaching.

Ted swallowed hard, his throat dry. "Where am I?" His voice cracked, barely more than a whisper.

Silence.

His eyes adjusted to the harsh lighting, and he dared to look around. The room was stark, industrial, the walls bare concrete stained with something dark. The scent of oil and decay clung to the air. A single metal tray stood nearby, its surface lined with carefully arranged tools—pliers, scalpels, a blowtorch, a hammer. Each one gleamed under the overhead light, polished and waiting.

Footsteps stopped just beyond his vision. Then, a voice—low, composed, utterly devoid of emotion.

"You're awake."

Ted twisted his neck, trying to catch sight of the speaker. A figure emerged from the shadows, moving with the slow, predatory grace of someone who had done this before. Jason.

"Who—" Ted's breath caught in his throat. He knew. The fear settled deeper, thick as tar. "What do you want?"

Jason remained silent for a moment, studying him. Then, he reached for the metal tray, his gloved fingers brushing against the tools.

Ted's body tensed. "Please," he croaked, his voice hoarse. "Whatever this is, whatever you're being paid—"

Jason finally spoke, his tone eerily calm. "It's not about money."

The room seemed to shrink around them. Ted could hear his own heartbeat, the erratic rhythm pounding against his eardrums. He tugged against the restraints again, desperate, knowing it was useless.

Jason picked up a pair of pliers, turning them over in his hands before meeting Ted's terrified gaze.

"We're going to have a conversation."

Chapter 6

The room was a tomb of steel and concrete, the air thick with the acrid stench of sweat, fear, and coppery blood. Fluorescent lights buzzed overhead, their sickly white glow flickering against the rust-streaked walls. The cold air carried a dampness that clung to the skin, making the exposed flesh feel clammy, as if death itself breathed in the room.

Jason stood over Ted, his movements deliberate, methodical. The restraints around Ted's wrists and ankles had long since bitten into his skin, leaving angry red welts where he had struggled in vain. The metal table beneath him was sticky with blood and sweat, the scent of it pungent, saturating every breath.

Jason reached into his pocket, retrieving a pair of industrial-grade earplugs. He rolled them between his fingers before pushing them deep into his ears. The world dulled instantly, Ted's panicked whimpers reduced to a distant murmur. Jason preferred it this way. He had learned long ago that screams could be distracting, that pleas for mercy could slip into the cracks of a man's mind if he let them. He had no use for distractions.

He picked up the scalpel first. The blade was sharp, pristine, catching the harsh light as he turned it in his gloved hand. He pressed the tip against Ted's forearm, just enough to break the skin, to let the first bead of crimson well up before it slid down, hot and slick, pooling at the table's edge.

Ted's body bucked instinctively, his muffled scream vibrating through the metal restraints. Jason watched the way the muscles in Ted's arm tensed, how his fingers curled into fists as the pain settled in. He dragged the scalpel in a slow, precise line down Ted's arm, the flesh splitting neatly apart. A fresh wave of blood seeped from the wound, the metallic scent rising thick into the stagnant air.

Jason set the scalpel down with care, exchanging it for a pair of forceps. He pinched the thin layer of skin at the edge of the incision and pulled. Ted's body jerked as Jason began peeling back the layers, his movements slow, deliberate. The wet, sticky sound of flesh separating from muscle filled the air, a sickening rip as Jason worked his way down, exposing the sinewy tissue beneath. Ted convulsed violently, his muffled screams growing desperate, but Jason didn't stop. Inch by inch, he flayed the arm, revealing the intricate network of muscle fibers and tendons beneath.

When he finally reached the exposed bone, Jason leaned in, examining his work with quiet fascination. Ted's arm was raw now, stripped of its protective layer, every nerve ending exposed to the biting chill of the air. Jason trailed a gloved finger over the exposed muscle, feeling its heat, its pulsing life beneath his touch.

He reached for the scalpel again.

With the precision of a surgeon, he traced the blade along one of the tendons running through the arm. Ted's body stiffened, his throat working in silent sobs beneath the gag as Jason pressed down, slowly slicing through the fibrous tissue. The tendon snapped back like a rubber band, retracting into the open wound, leaving the arm limp, useless. The sound was thick, wet, visceral. Jason tilted his head, watching the way Ted's fingers twitched involuntarily, how his body spasmed at the loss of function.

Satisfied, he set the blade aside and reached for a small glass jar.

Salt.

He took a pinch between his fingers and let the grains sprinkle onto the raw, exposed muscle. The reaction was immediate—Ted's back arched violently, his entire body convulsing against the restraints, his throat tearing itself raw in a scream that Jason barely registered through the earplugs. The salt seeped into every open wound, every exposed nerve, sending fresh waves of agony coursing through his ruined arm.

Jason watched, his expression unreadable, as Ted trembled uncontrollably, his body slick with sweat and blood. The scent of iron and raw flesh thickened, filling every breath, saturating the air with the unmistakable stench of suffering.

He exhaled slowly, stretching his fingers before reaching for the next tool.

The hammer.

Ted was shaking now, his body reduced to a quivering, broken mess. Jason studied him for a moment, watching the shallow rise and fall of his chest, the way his fingers twitched involuntarily. He wondered if Ted even had the strength to fight anymore.

He lifted the hammer, angling it over Ted's knee, and brought it down in a single, brutal arc.

Crack.

The bone shattered beneath the force, the vibration traveling up Jason's arm as the hammer connected. The sound was unmistakable—wet, splintering, followed by the muted wail that managed to pierce through even the earplugs. Jason waited, watching as Ted's chest heaved, his head lolling to the side, barely conscious.

He reached into his bag and retrieved a syringe, tapping the side before pressing the needle into Ted's thigh. The adrenaline surged instantly, forcing Ted's body back from the brink, his eyes snapping open in renewed horror. Jason tilted his head, watching him.

"Can't have you checking out on me yet."

The room was ripe with suffering—burnt flesh, fresh blood, sweat, and the lingering tang of fear. Jason inhaled deeply, then exhaled through his nose, rolling his shoulders as he prepared for the next round.

After all, he wasn't finished yet.

"You're going to help me," Jason continued. "You get to choose what happens next."

Ted's fingers curled into fists. "Choose?" he rasped, his throat dry. "What kind of sick game is this?"

Jason crouched beside him, resting his forearms on his knees. "It's simple," he murmured. "You decide what I use first." He gestured toward the tray of instruments. "Scalpel? Hammer? Blowtorch? Or should we start with something less... final?"

Ted's breath hitched. His mind screamed at him to fight, to break free, but the cold reality of the restraints held him down. His body was shaking, sweat pooling at the nape of his neck despite the chill in the air.

"I won't play this," Ted whispered.

Jason's expression didn't change, but there was a flicker of something—amusement, perhaps.

"That's the thing," he said, voice barely above a whisper. "You already are."

Without waiting for an answer, Jason pressed the scalpel against Ted's forearm, the blade cool against his skin. "Shallow," Jason murmured, dragging the tip ever so lightly, barely breaking the surface. "Or deep? You tell me."

Ted clenched his jaw. "Go to hell."

Jason smiled, though it didn't reach his eyes. "I've been there," he said, pressing just hard enough for a thin line of blood to bead along the cut. "It's not as different from here as you might think."

Then, with a flick of his wrist, he drove the scalpel deeper, slicing into the muscle. Ted's scream echoed off the cold walls, his back arching instinctively against the restraints. Pain, sharp and immediate, tore through his arm, the sensation of flesh parting beneath the blade a grotesque revelation of fragility.

Jason worked efficiently, his movements precise. The scalpel left a jagged, deliberate gash before he wiped the blade against his gloved hand. "See?" he murmured. "That wasn't so bad."

Ted gasped, his vision blurring at the edges, nausea twisting his stomach.

Jason reached into his kit and pulled out a syringe filled with clear liquid. He tapped it once before plunging it into Ted's thigh. The effect was near-instantaneous—his body jolted, the burning rush of adrenaline surging through his veins, forcing him back from the brink of unconsciousness.

"We're just getting started," Jason said.

Next was the blowtorch.

Jason flicked the igniter, the blue-orange flame casting a flickering glow on Ted's skin. The air grew thick with the acrid scent of burning flesh as Jason lowered the flame to Ted's arm, the skin blistering and blackening in mere seconds. Ted's screams turned hoarse, his body writhing in agony as the fire seared into him, the unbearable heat sinking deep into his nerves.

"Shhh," Jason whispered, almost soothingly. "You're still with me."

Another syringe. Another forced jolt of consciousness.

The pliers followed. Jason took his time, gripping one of Ted's fingernails and twisting, the resistance giving way before the nail tore free with a sickening pop. Ted's voice broke, raw and ragged, his entire body slick with sweat and pain.

Jason sighed, wiping a gloved hand over his brow as he admired his work. "You're doing well," he said, almost encouragingly. "Most people would've checked out by now."

Ted's head lolled to the side, his eyes half-lidded, his breath coming in rapid, shallow bursts. Jason gave him one final injection, ensuring he wouldn't slip away just yet.

Then he leaned in, his voice barely a whisper against Ted's ear.

"Let's see how much more you can take."

Chapter 7

The air in the room was thick with the acrid scent of burnt flesh, blood, and sweat. Ted's body trembled involuntarily, his breath coming in ragged gasps. The pain was everywhere—raw and unrelenting, his nerves flayed open with every throb. His body no longer felt like his own, just a collection of searing wounds held together by agony and the forced clarity of adrenaline. His mind teetered on the edge of oblivion, but Jason wouldn't let him slip away.

Jason stood at the edge of the table, regarding his work with an unreadable expression. His gloved hands were stained with crimson, streaks of dried blood darkening the creases of his fingers. He exhaled slowly, tilting his head, as if assessing whether Ted could endure another round.

Ted barely registered movement when Jason leaned in, his voice low, almost conversational.

"You've done well," he murmured. "Better than I expected."

Ted's cracked lips parted, his voice barely a whisper. "Please... no more."

Jason's lips twitched into something resembling a smirk. "No more?" He gestured around the room, to the scattered tools, the blood-streaked surface of the table, the charred skin along one of Ted's arm. "We're past that point, don't you think?"

Ted's eyes were glazed with exhaustion, pain swallowing every other thought, but somewhere deep in his gut, anger still simmered beneath the surface. He wanted to scream, to curse, to spit in Jason's face—but his body no longer had the strength to act on his rage.

Jason sighed and, for the first time, stepped away. The shift in his posture was almost casual, as if his interest in the game had started to wane. He set the hammer down with a dull clunk, wiped his hands on a towel, and rolled his shoulders.

"I think you've had enough," he said, walking toward a small cabinet at the back of the room. He retrieved a single syringe, tapping it lightly with his fingers. The liquid inside shimmered under the harsh fluorescent light. "A reward, perhaps?"

Ted tried to focus, blinking against the sweat and blood clinging to his lashes. "What... what is that?"

Jason chuckled. "Mercy."

For the first time in hours, a tiny ember of hope flickered in Ted's chest. He had resigned himself to death, convinced that this basement room would be his tomb, but now—now Jason was offering him something different. His fractured mind clung to the possibility, desperate to believe in even the faintest chance of escape. Maybe it was finally over. Maybe Jason had gotten his fill, had grown bored, and would end this twisted game.

His breathing steadied, though weak, as he watched Jason approach with the syringe. He tried to imagine himself outside of this nightmare—free, alive, walking down a quiet street, feeling the sun on his skin, holding Emily in his arms again. He wanted to believe. He had to believe.

The needle pierced his arm, a sharp, fleeting sting. The liquid burned as it entered his bloodstream, spreading through him like wildfire. A moment later, his body went slack, his muscles unable to respond.

Panic gripped him as he realised the truth—this was no mercy. His mind was still sharp, still screaming, but his body had been stolen from him. He couldn't lift his arms, couldn't move his legs. He was paralysed, a prisoner in his own skin.

Jason leaned in close, whispering against his ear. "You're not dying, Ted. Not yet." He tapped a finger against the metal restraints. "Just loosening the leash."

Ted's limbs felt foreign, disconnected from his mind, as if submerged in thick tar. He could still feel everything—every wound, every break, every pulsing ache—but he couldn't move. Couldn't fight. Couldn't even flinch as Jason reached down and unfastened one of the leather straps securing his leg.

Jason straightened and stepped back, watching Ted carefully. But there was no satisfaction in his gaze, no triumph. He didn't savour the fear in Ted's eyes or the way his body lay limp and useless on the table. There was only detachment—cold, clinical, as if he were simply finishing a task that had long lost its meaning.

The rush, the fire, the purpose that had once filled Jason in moments like these was gone. There was no pleasure in the suffering anymore, no thrill in the power he held over another man's fate. He had expected to feel something when he saw the light dim in Ted's eyes, some spark of fulfilment, but there was nothing. Just silence. Just emptiness.

Jason turned toward the door, flicking off the light as he left.

Darkness swallowed the room, and for the first time, Ted was truly alone with his pain.

Chapter 8

Darkness clung to Ted, suffocating him as he lay motionless on the cold metal table, his limbs unresponsive, his breathing shallow. The paralytic coursing through his veins held him in a cruel stasis—awake, aware, but utterly helpless. His mind screamed at his body to move, to run, to fight, but he was trapped within his own flesh, a prisoner of Jason's twisted game.

The minutes stretched into eternity. The silence was deafening, the only sound his own ragged breathing and the distant, mechanical drip of water from a leaking pipe somewhere beyond his field of vision. The darkness was absolute, but Ted could still feel the burning agony radiating from his battered body. Every nerve was alight with pain, a cruel reminder that he was still alive.

Then, something changed.

A faint tingling sensation pricked at his fingertips. A subtle shift in the weight of his limbs. His breath caught in his throat—was the paralytic wearing off? The thought was both exhilarating and terrifying. If Jason returned too soon, he would be helpless once more. But if he was patient, if he waited just long enough...

He focused, willing his fingers to move. It started as the barest twitch, a ghost of sensation, then grew stronger. His wrists ached, raw from the restraints, but he felt the subtle give in the loosened strap around his leg. Jason had left it undone. A mistake? Or another sick game?

Ted didn't care.

With every ounce of effort, he flexed his toes, then his ankle. The freedom was intoxicating, but he forced himself to move slowly, cautiously. He couldn't risk alerting Jason if he was still nearby. He inhaled deeply, bracing against the pain, and turned his leg just enough to slip free of the restraint.

His heart pounded. He was close.

With painstaking effort, he worked his arm loose next. The metal buckle scraped against his burned skin, sending fresh jolts of pain shooting through him, but he bit back the scream threatening to rise. He wouldn't give Jason the satisfaction.

Finally, he was free.

Ted slid off the table, his bare feet hitting the concrete floor with a dull slap. His legs buckled, the sheer exhaustion of his torment nearly sending him crashing down, but he steadied himself. His breath came in sharp gasps, his body protesting every movement. He had no time to recover—he needed to move.

He stumbled toward the door, his hands fumbling against the smooth, cold surface. His fingers found the handle. He turned it slowly, so slowly, willing it not to creak.

The door opened.

His breath hitched. He was out.

But something was wrong.

The corridor beyond was too dark, too empty. The air was thick with a tension that made the hairs on the back of his neck rise. The only illumination came from a single flickering light overhead, casting shadows that twisted and writhed like living things.

Ted took a shaky step forward, his heart hammering in his chest. Each movement was agony, but he pushed forward, dragging himself down the hall. His body screamed for rest, but his mind screamed louder.

Then he heard it.

Footsteps.

Slow. Measured. Coming from somewhere ahead.

His blood turned to ice.

Jason's voice drifted through the darkness, calm, almost amused. "You really thought it would be that easy?"

Ted's breath hitched. He turned, his instincts screaming for him to run, but the moment he moved, the overhead light clicked off, plunging the corridor into absolute blackness.

Then came the sound.

The unmistakable metallic slide of a knife being drawn from its sheath.

Jason was toying with him. Letting him taste freedom, only to snatch it away at the last second.

Ted swallowed hard, forcing himself to take another step back. The pain, the exhaustion, the fear—it was all irrelevant now. He had one chance. One.

He ran.

The hallway was a labyrinth of shadows and unseen dangers, but Ted didn't care. His pulse roared in his ears, his legs barely carrying him forward. He stumbled, crashed into the wall, but kept going. The sound of Jason's footsteps followed, unhurried, steady, as if he had all the time in the world.

Ted rounded a corner, gasping for breath. There—at the end of the hall, a door. An exit. Salvation.

He threw himself forward, his hands reaching for the handle, desperation fuelling his final lunge.

A searing pain ripped through his side.

Ted choked on a cry, his knees buckling as he crumpled against the door. His trembling hands lifted, pressing against the burning wound at his ribs. Warm blood oozed between his fingers.

Jason's voice was right behind him now, low and mocking. "You almost made it."

Ted tried to turn, to fight, but Jason's hands were already on him, dragging him back into the darkness.

The last thing Ted saw was the exit sign flickering above him, taunting him with its promise of freedom.

Then, the darkness swallowed him whole.

Chapter 9:

The world was a blur of pain and fading consciousness. Ted barely felt himself being dragged through the darkness, his body limp, his breath shallow. Blood dripped from the wound in his side, leaving a smeared trail along the cold concrete floor. The escape had been an illusion, a cruel trick played by a man who had perfected the art of control.

Jason moved with the same slow, methodical pace as ever, unbothered by the weight of the man in his grip. The door to the torture room creaked open again, the familiar sterile light stabbing into Ted's barely functioning vision. He was thrown unceremoniously onto the cold metal table, a groan escaping his cracked lips as the restraints were refastened around his wrists and ankles. There would be no more attempts to run.

Jason stood over him, staring down with an expression that was unreadable. Gone was the amusement, the toying interest that had once lingered in his voice. Now there was only a quiet finality. He exhaled slowly, as if letting go of some unseen burden, and reached for the tray of instruments beside him.

"You fought well," Jason murmured, selecting a blade and running his gloved fingers along the edge. "Better than most."

Ted could barely lift his head, his voice a raw whisper. "Why… why do this?"

Jason paused, as if considering his answer. Then he let out a sigh, one that carried no satisfaction, no malice. "Because it's what I do now."

He pressed the knife against Ted's throat, letting the cold steel linger against his burning skin. Ted felt no fear anymore—only exhaustion, only the slow acceptance of what was to come. He thought he would feel something—panic, anger, regret—but instead, it was as if he were floating, his mind drifting further and further away, like a cloud detached from the sky. The pain was a distant thing now, like a fading echo of a life that no longer belonged to him. The air around him felt lighter, weightless.

Jason hesitated, just for a second, before slicing cleanly across Ted's throat. The pain was brief, a sharp bloom before it faded into nothing. Blood spilled onto the table, pooling beneath his head. His body twitched once, then stilled.

Jason stepped back, watching the life drain from the man he had stalked, tormented, and finally ended. The room was silent again. Yet, instead of satisfaction, Jason felt... nothing. No rush, no weight lifted, no closure. The act was mechanical, rehearsed—just a job.

His chest felt empty, hollow, as though he were merely an observer to the scene before him rather than the architect of its outcome. The moment stretched, the silence thick and suffocating. The body on the table was just another finished piece, another blank space in the long string of names he will erase. Jason felt himself slipping further away from whatever remnants of humanity he had, yet was powerless to stop it.

Without another word, he set the knife down and began the meticulous process of cleaning up. He worked mechanically, wiping down surfaces, disposing of evidence, moving with a precision that spoke to experience. Bleach burned the scent of blood from the air, plastic sheeting wrapped around the cooling body, and by the time Jason was done, the room looked almost untouched.

He paused for a moment, glancing at Ted's lifeless face beneath the plastic. There was no pleasure in the kill, no thrill. Just a job finished. A name crossed off the list.

Jason picked up the tape recorder from the table and pressed stop.

The final act was complete.

And yet, as he stood there, staring at what remained, the emptiness inside him stretched, vast and unending. He had done what needed to be done, but he was no closer to feeling whole.

He never would be.

Chapter 10

Jason sat in the dim glow of his apartment, the city's neon lights casting shifting colours across the walls through the blinds. The scent of bleach still clung to his skin despite his best efforts to wash it away. The job was done. Ted Monroe was gone. The warehouse was clean. And yet, as Jason stared at the small package in front of him, he felt nothing.

The tape.

A recording of Ted's final moments, his last cries, his futile resistance before the inevitable. It sat there, silent, waiting to be sent to the client. Proof of completion. A payment transaction sealed in suffering.

Jason picked up the package, weighing it in his hands. It wasn't the money that bothered him — he never cared for it beyond necessity. The weight of the task lingered in his chest, but it was a hollow thing. He had thought, maybe, that this would feel different. That something inside him would shift. But didn't.

He slipped the package into a padded envelope, scrawled an unmarked address onto the front, and sealed it.

By morning, it would be delivered. A name erased. A transaction complete. The first of many.

He poured himself a glass of whiskey, the amber liquid catching the glow of the city outside. He took a slow sip, letting the burn settle in his throat, but it did nothing to thaw the cold inside him. His fingers traced the rim of the glass as he stared at the scattered files on his table—potential contracts, faces of the living soon to be dead.

The next job awaited.

Jason leaned back, exhaling a breath he didn't know he had been holding. He had long since stopped questioning why he continued. Why the abyss still called to him. It was a cycle—one kill after another, names replaced by new ones, faces blurred into the next. But in the spaces between, in the silence that stretched longer each time, the weight pressed heavier.

He finished his drink and stood, grabbing one of the folders from the pile. Another contract. Another life waiting to be taken.

Tomorrow, he would begin again.

Chapter 11

Jason had always known that past contracts could come back to haunt him. It was part of the job—kill, erase, move forward. But as he flipped open the latest file on his desk, a sinking feeling settled deep in his chest.

The client was named Mark Holloway, a man with sharp features and a stare that carried the weight of a vendetta. He was requesting a hit on Melanie Carter.

Jason's fingers tensed around the file. Melanie. The name sent a cold ripple down his spine. Ted Monroe's ex-wife.

He scanned the details. Mark Holloway was the brother of a man Jason didn't recognise—David Holloway, a former business partner of Melanie's late husband. The report claimed David had died under questionable circumstances, just like several other men connected to Melanie over the years. She had a pattern—legal battles, financial ruin, and then sudden deaths that no one could quite prove were linked to her.

She was smart. Careful. Always finding a new way to manipulate, always covering her tracks. And most importantly, she never used the same hitman twice.

Jason swallowed hard, his pulse a steady drum in his ears.

He had been her latest choice.

Ted Monroe had never been a villain. He had been another victim.

Jason closed the file, breathing through the slow burn of realisation. He had taken the contract blindly, believing the version of the story Melanie had provided. She had framed Ted as a controlling, abusive man, desperate to keep his daughter under his thumb. But now, the pieces were shifting, rearranging themselves into something far more sinister.

Melanie Carter had orchestrated everything.

Jason rose from his chair, his muscles rigid. He had been played. Used. And Ted Monroe had died because of it.

For the first time in years, Jason felt something gnaw at him—not guilt exactly, but a weight that wasn't so easily dismissed. He had prided himself on making the right calls, choosing targets who deserved the bullet or the blade. But now? Now he was just another pawn in someone else's game.

And it was too late to undo it.

The contract on Melanie was still active. Holloway wanted her dead for what she had done to his brother. Jason could take the job. It would be clean, precise, just like all the others.

But it wouldn't bring Ted Monroe back.

Jason exhaled sharply, his grip tightening around the file. This was different. This wasn't just a contract anymore. This was something personal.

For the first time in his career, Jason wasn't sure if he was going to complete the job.

Chapter 12

The auction had been discreet, a private affair held in the basement of a crumbling estate outside of the city. A gathering of collectors, historians, and those who found pleasure in the relics of suffering. Jason had attended with a singular purpose—acquiring something that had long fascinated him: a scold's bridle.

A cruel device from the past, used to silence those deemed disruptive—most often women accused of gossip, treason, or witchcraft. A metal cage designed to wrap around the head, with a sharp plate that forced its way into the mouth, rendering the wearer unable to speak, unable to scream.

He had outbid a man who had wanted it for display. Jason had wanted it for something else entirely.

Now, it had a purpose.

Jason sat in the dim light of his apartment, the file on Melanie Carter still open before him. His fingers traced the edges of the paper, his mind already decided. He had been used, deceived, and made a tool in her twisted game. Now, he would be the instrument of her end.

The plan was already forming in his mind. It would not be swift. It would not be clean.

It would be justice.

Melanie Carter awoke bound to the same table where Ted Monroe had died, the scent of blood and scorched flesh still thick in the air. Her wrists and ankles were strapped down, her body vulnerable. Panic bloomed in her eyes as she struggled, testing the restraints.
Jason stood over Melanie, his expression unreadable as he slowly removed his gloves, one finger at a time, savoring the quiet before the storm. The room was dimly lit, the single flickering bulb casting shadows that crawled across the stained concrete walls. The scent of

sweat, fear, and old blood thickened the air, clinging to the back of Jason's throat like a promise yet to be fulfilled.

Melanie was bound tightly to the steel table, her wrists and ankles raw from struggling against the leather restraints. Her breath came in ragged bursts, panic thick in her wide, tear-streaked eyes as she tried to shake her head, tried to plead past the cloth gag stuffing her mouth.

Jason crouched beside her, his voice disturbingly calm. "I want you to understand what's about to happen," he said, tapping his fingers against the metal tray of tools beside him. "I think it's only fair, given all the stories you spun, all the little games you played."

Her muffled sobs grew louder, her body trembling beneath him. He ignored it, continuing as if she hadn't made a sound.

"You like control, don't you, Melanie?" He plucked a scalpel from the tray, rolling it between his fingers. "You like pulling the strings, making people dance to whatever little narrative you construct. Ted was just another piece on your board, another pawn in your game. And me? I was the fool who carried out your dirty work."

He leaned in closer, his breath warm against her ear. "But you underestimated me."

He stood back up, straightening his shoulders as he placed the scalpel down and picked up something else—a rusted, archaic metal contraption, its jagged edges worn with time but no less cruel.

"This," he said, holding it up for her to see, "is a scold's bridle. It was used centuries ago to silence women accused of spreading lies, deceit, and manipulation. Fitting, don't you think?"

Melanie's eyes widened in horror, her entire body convulsing in frantic, jerky movements. She shook her head wildly, trying to scream past the gag, but Jason merely chuckled.

"Oh, don't worry. That's just the beginning."

He set the bridle down gently, as if it were delicate, before reaching for a small steel box. "Next, I'm going to introduce you to some old friends of mine." He clicked open the box's latches, revealing a collection of writhing, starved rats. Their tiny claws scraped against the metal, their noses twitching, already sensing fresh meat.

Melanie's entire body jerked against the restraints, a high-pitched, terrified wail escaping past the gag. Jason watched her, tilting his head like a predator studying wounded prey.

"You see, rats are remarkable creatures," he mused, setting the box aside for now. "They'll do anything to survive, even eat through flesh if they have no other option." He gestured to the heavy metal bucket on the tray. "I'll strap this to your stomach, put a few of my little friends inside, and then apply some heat. They won't have anywhere to go... except through you."

A fresh wave of terror passed through Melanie's eyes, her pupils blown wide with raw, unfiltered panic. She thrashed violently, her muffled screams desperate, primal.

Jason let out a sudden burst of laughter, sharp and cruel, as he stepped back, crossing his arms. "Actually... let's make this fun." He gestured toward the tools and grinned. "You pick."

Melanie whimpered, her entire body shuddering as her eyes darted wildly over the instruments of pain. Jason gave her a moment, watching the sweat bead on her forehead, her breathing growing shallower.

"No answer?" he mocked, leaning against the table. "Oh, come on, Melanie. You controlled so much, ruined so many lives. And now, faced with a real choice, you go silent?"

She squeezed her eyes shut, sobbing through the gag. Jason threw his head back, laughing hard, the sound echoing in the small, suffocating room. "That's priceless," he wheezed, wiping his eyes. "Ted screamed too, you know. But at least he had the balls to beg."

He picked up the scalpel and dragged the cold steel along the exposed skin of her arm, pressing just hard enough to break the skin. Melanie seized up, a choked gurgle escaping her throat. The cut wasn't deep—just enough to let the blood bead before trickling down in a slow, lazy path.

"You feel that?" Jason whispered. "That's nothing. That's a tickle compared to what's coming."

He set the blade aside and grabbed the scold's bridle, fastening the rusted metal around her head. The jagged mouthpiece pressed against her tongue, forcing her jaw wide open. Drool and muffled, incoherent cries dripped from the corners of her lips as she writhed in agony.

Jason leaned in, his voice dark. "Ted thought he could reason with me. He thought if he gave up, I'd let him go. But I made him watch as I peeled away his skin, layer by layer. You're going to get the same, Melanie. Because unlike Ted, you actually deserve this."

Melanie's body convulsed violently, her eyes rolling back, her muffled screams raw and desperate. Jason only grinned, lifting the metal bucket.

"Let's see how long it takes before they start chewing."

Her body shuddered as the rats burrowed deeper, squealing and thrashing within the confined space of the box. Her fingers curled into fists, her nails biting into her own palms as pain eclipsed every other thought.

Jason straightened, inhaling deeply. The air reeked of burned flesh and blood, the scent thick enough to cling to his lungs. He turned and reached for the blade.

In a single motion, he sliced through her tongue, severing the muscle cleanly. Blood spurted, dark and viscous, as her choked screams rattled through the iron restraint. Her body shook violently, thrashing against the table, but there was no mercy here.

Jason wiped the blade against his sleeve, watching as Melanie's eyes lost focus, the pain dragging her toward the edge of oblivion. He crouched beside her, his voice steady, almost soothing.

"I wonder," he said softly, "if the others begged like this. The ones you set up before Ted. Did they scream for you? Did you watch as the light left their eyes?"

Her body spasmed again, but she had no words left. No defence. Just agony.

By the time her body went still, the rats had burrowed deep, and the stench of burnt flesh and blood filled the room.

Jason exhaled, setting the blade down beside her ruined form.

This was no contract.

This was retribution.

Chapter 13

The humid air of Bogotá clung to Jason like a second skin as he stepped onto the balcony of his rented apartment. The city sprawled beneath him, a mixture of wealth and desperation, modern skyscrapers and crumbling slums pressing against each other like uneasy partners in a dance. Here, he was nobody—just another foreigner seeking anonymity in a place where people rarely asked questions.

He took a slow drag from his cigarette, exhaling a thin stream of smoke into the thick night air. The lights of the city flickered below, but Jason's mind was far away. The weight of his past still clung to him, the echoes of Ted Monroe's screams, the final gurgling sobs of Melanie Carter. He had thought that killing her would bring closure, but instead, it had only driven him further into the void.

Trust was a dangerous thing. Melanie had proven that. He had allowed himself to believe her, to take her word as truth, and it had cost an innocent man his life. It had cost Jason something, too—whatever shreds of morality he had been clinging to.

He couldn't let that happen again.

The job had always been simple—kill, clean, disappear. No emotion, no attachments, no second thoughts. But now, the lines had blurred. He had let himself become a weapon for the wrong cause.

He couldn't afford that weakness again.

Jason turned back inside, locking the balcony doors behind him. The apartment was sparse—just a bed, a table, a single chair. A duffel bag sat open on the floor, filled with cash, fake passports, and the tools of his trade. He had no ties here, no connections. South America was a temporary hiding place, a pause before the next move.

Because there would be a next move.

He was good at what he did. Killing was a skill, and skills needed to be honed. But this time, he would be smarter. More careful. He would never be manipulated again, never let someone else's lies steer him toward an undeserved kill.

The world was vast, full of people who needed men like him—men who could erase problems, silence threats, restore balance in the darkest ways. He would find them, and he would do what he did best.

Jason zipped the duffel bag shut, slinging it over his shoulder.

The rainforest stretched ahead of him like an endless emerald sea, thick with life and mystery. He had left the city behind, trading its suffocating crowds for the deep solitude of the jungle. Each step he took along the muddy trail was swallowed by the hum of unseen creatures, the distant calls of birds echoing through the dense canopy above. The air smelled of damp earth, the rich scent of moss and decay mingling with the sharp tang of wild orchids.

It reminded him of the stories he used to tell Lily.

The explorer who ventured deep into the jungle, the brave adventurer who mapped the hidden places of the world. He had spun tales of ancient ruins covered in vines, of rivers teeming with golden fish, of creatures who lurked just beyond the trees, watching, waiting.

"Tell me another, Daddy," she had whispered, curled up in bed, eyes wide with wonder.

Jason swallowed hard, pushing the memory away. But the jungle wouldn't let him forget. Every rustling leaf, every shifting shadow brought those nights back to him—the warmth of her small body tucked against his side, the soft rise and fall of her breathing as she drifted to sleep.

He had told her those stories to make her feel safe, to make her believe the world was full of magic and adventure.

Now, he walked through that same world, but there was no magic here. Only the endless green, the damp heat pressing against his skin, the knowledge that there was no one left to listen to his stories..

Towering ceiba trees loomed overhead, their immense roots twisting through the undergrowth like the limbs of ancient giants. Vines hung in tangled webs, some thick enough to support his weight, others delicate and laced with tiny blossoms in hues of violet and crimson.

A flash of movement caught his eye—a capuchin monkey darting through the branches, its curious gaze following him for a moment before vanishing into the leaves. Nearby, a butterfly with iridescent blue wings fluttered lazily past, its colours shimmering in the dappled sunlight that broke through gaps in the canopy.

Jason inhaled deeply, feeling the humidity cling to his skin, soaking through his clothes. He walked with no real destination, just needing to move, to let the jungle's vastness swallow him. Here, there was no city noise, no whispers of his past creeping in. The rainforest was indifferent to him—it lived, thrived, and decayed without regard for men like him.

He stopped at the edge of a slow-moving river, the water dark, its surface shifting with unseen currents. A caiman lay half-submerged near the far bank, its reptilian eyes unblinking, patient. Jason watched it for a moment, admiring its stillness, its effortless predation. A creature that killed because it had to, not because it questioned morality or sought vengeance.

He crouched down, trailing his fingers through the cool water, letting the sensation ground him. The rainforest didn't care about his past, his regrets, or his future. It simply was.

Maybe that was what he needed to be, too.

Jason stood, exhaling slowly, and turned back toward the trail.

It was time to disappear, to refocus, to become untouchable.

And this time, he would trust no one.

Chapter 14

Jason walked deeper into the rainforest, the weight of his past dragging at his heels like a ghost refusing to let go. The air was thick with the scent of damp earth and decay, the sounds of the jungle wrapping around him in a symphony of unseen life. The further he walked, the clearer his thoughts became. For the first time in years, he found himself considering a different path.

Maybe there was still a way forward that didn't end in blood. Maybe the skills that had made him a ghost, a killer, could be turned toward something better. He had spent years hunting men, ending lives, being used as a weapon for people like Melanie Carter—people who preyed on the weak, manipulating those around them for their own gain.

But what if he turned the game on its head? What if, instead of being a tool for the corrupt, he hunted those who truly deserved it? The traffickers, the slavers, the men who built their wealth on the suffering of others. The world was full of them. Here, in the heart of South

America, such men thrived in the shadows, untouched by law and justice.

Jason exhaled slowly, feeling something shift inside him. For the first time in a long time, he felt purpose beyond a paycheque, beyond survival. This could be something real. Something meaningful.

The thought gave him energy, pushing him forward, step by step, back toward the city.

Then, he felt it.

A sharp sting against his ankle.

Jason frowned and glanced down, brushing absently at his leg. A few small black ants scurried away, their bites irritating but nothing serious. He took another step, but a sudden, burning pain shot through his foot, crawling up his leg like fire beneath his skin.

He stumbled.

More stings. Dozens. Then hundreds.

His breath caught in his throat as he realised what was happening. The ground beneath him writhed with movement, the dirt itself alive with a river of black bodies. Army ants.

Jason tried to move, but his body was already weakening. He had seen what these creatures could do—strip an animal to the bone in hours. He had never imagined he would be their next victim.

He fell to his knees, his pulse pounding in his ears. The bites came in waves, a relentless tide of agony. The swarm covered him, climbing his legs, burrowing beneath his clothes, sinking their tiny, merciless jaws into his flesh. His vision blurred as his body went into shock, every nerve screaming in protest.

Then the horror truly began.

The ants did not simply bite; they invaded. Jason could feel them forcing their way beneath his skin, slipping into his nostrils, crawling into his ears, writhing behind his eyes. His screams shattered the stillness of the jungle, but the only answer was the endless chittering of the swarm. His muscles seized as the pain reached deeper, fire consuming him from the inside out.

He clawed at his skin, ripping deep furrows into his flesh as he tried to dislodge them. But for every one he crushed, a hundred more took its place. His fingers twisted into claws, digging at his own body as if he could tear them free, but they had already burrowed too deep. His insides writhed, a sickening sensation of movement beneath his skin as the ants ate him alive from within.

His stomach convulsed violently, bile rising in his throat as he felt them inside his mouth, gnawing at his gums, his tongue, his throat. He choked, gagged, tried to spit them out, but his lungs burned as they crawled into his windpipe, choking off his breath. The pain was unimaginable, a suffering beyond anything he had inflicted in his years of killing.

His body convulsed in the dirt, foam flecking his lips, his limbs spasming uncontrollably. The heat of the jungle wrapped around him like a suffocating embrace, pressing down as his vision darkened. The world blurred, the shapes of the trees twisting into shadows as his mind fractured under the unbearable torment.

His last thought was bitter, cruelly ironic.

He had decided to change. To help. To do something good.

And the jungle had swallowed him whole before he even had the chance.

The rainforest hummed around him, indifferent. The ants continued their work, dismantling him piece by piece. By the time the sun set, Jason was nothing more than another story lost in the wild.

Epilogue

Jason had always believed death would be the end. Darkness, silence, nothingness. But he was wrong.

He didn't move on. He didn't fade. He lingered, tethered to the ones he had left behind—not the ones who knew his name, but the ones who had suffered because of him.

He saw them all.

The families of the men and women he had executed. The daughters waiting at the window, their small hands pressed against the glass, eyes searching for a father who would never come home. The mothers who still set an extra place at the dinner table, unable to admit that their son's seat would forever remain empty. The wives who slept with the TV on, the static hum of background noise the only thing keeping them from listening to the silence of an empty bed.

And he could do nothing.

Jason was a spectre, a shadow trapped between the living and the void. He drifted through their homes, unseen, unheard. He screamed, he begged, he howled at the walls of his prison, but his words dissolved into nothing. They would never know he was there. They would never hear his apologies, his regret, his agony.

But he could hear them.

Every whispered prayer, every sob in the darkness, every desperate plea.

"Please come home."

"I know you're out there, baby. Just call me."

"The police are still looking. They'll find him, I know they will."

Jason watched as they scoured the streets, putting up posters with faces he could never forget, faces he had seen in their final moments. He stood over them as they clutched at old shirts, breathing in the fading scent of a man who was nothing but bones now. He sat at the edge of a little girl's bed as she told herself, over and over, that her daddy was just on a long trip, that he'd be home in time for her birthday.

He saw their hope. And he saw it die.

Days turned to months. Some accepted the truth with quiet devastation, folding away old clothes into boxes, deleting phone numbers they could no longer bear to dial. Others refused, their obsession festering, turning their homes into shrines.

He followed a woman who refused to believe her husband was dead. She scoured every missing person's forum, visited every morgue, paid psychics to tell her lies. She muttered his name in her sleep, clutched a picture of him to her chest, whispered into the darkness, *"I know you're out there. Just tell me where you are."*

Jason wanted to scream the truth into her ear, to shake her, to force her to see. But he was nothing. A silent ghost shackled to the grief he had created.

And the worst part?

He wasn't alone.

In the deepest parts of the night, when the walls between the living and the dead were thinnest, he saw them—shadows like him, phantoms bound to their sins. Men who had taken lives, now forced to watch the destruction they had left behind, condemned to an eternity of regret.

Some had gone mad, repeating the names of their victims in endless mantras. Others wept, their agony seeping into the air like rot. Jason tried to ignore them, but their whispers crawled into his ears, their suffering a mirror of his own.

But then there were the angry ones. The ones who fought against the chains of their damnation, raging at the unseen forces that bound them. Jason watched as they tried, again and again, to reach into the world of the living— to push a glass from a table, to flicker a light, to carve a message into fogged-up mirrors. But it was useless. They were powerless. Just ghosts, forever screaming into the void.

Jason didn't know how long he had been there. Time had lost meaning. The weight of his sins grew heavier with every passing day, every cry he couldn't answer, every family he couldn't comfort.

He stood in the cold, dark room of a teenage boy, a son left fatherless by his hands. The boy whispered to a framed picture, tears streaking his face. *"I'll make you proud, Dad. I promise."* Jason reached out, wanting to stop him, to tell him the truth—that the world didn't reward good men, that there was no justice. But his fingers passed through the air like smoke.

This was his eternity.

Not fire, not brimstone.

Just an endless cycle of grief, regret, and silence.

Jason had spent his life killing. Now, he would spend forever watching life slip through his fingers, never able to touch it again.

And somewhere in the black abyss, laughter echoed—a cruel, unseen force delighting in his torment. The only thing worse than knowing he could never escape was the knowledge that something else was watching, feeding off his suffering, waiting for him to break.

The Witch's Name

Chapter 1

The iron hissed as it met her flesh, a sound lost beneath the echoing cries that filled the stone chamber.

The girl's body jerked, the restraints digging into her wrists and ankles as she writhed. The scent of burning skin thickened the air, mingling with the damp, mouldy stench of the underground prison.

The magistrate stood still, his face impassive, watching the scene unfold with all the interest of a man inspecting cattle at market. He shifted slightly as the inquisitor pulled back the glowing iron, revealing the blistered imprint of a cross upon the girl's forearm.

"You will confess." he said, his voice calm despite the screaming.

The girl panted, her face damp with sweat and tears. Her dark eyes flickered toward the magistrate, filled not with submission, but with fury.

"I am no witch," she rasped.

"We have many ways to make you talk, witch"
the magistrate said quietly, turning to the
inquisitor nodding to ready the next implement.

The first crack from the thumb screws came
with a blinding, white-hot agony.

Bone splintered. A sickening crunch echoed
through the stone chamber, reverberating off
the damp walls. The pain shot up her arm like
fire, raw and merciless, tearing through flesh,
through muscle, through everything that made
her human.

She screamed.

The magistrate did not flinch. Nor did the crowd
gathered before her, their faces masks of quiet
fascination.

"Again," the magistrate ordered.

The inquisitor obliged.

The screw turned once more, grinding against her already broken thumb, forcing the jagged remains of bone to shift beneath her skin. The pressure was unbearable, worse than any wound, worse than any burn. It was inside her, destroying her from within.

She could not see her hand anymore, only the cruel iron vice that swallowed her fingers whole. She could not tell where flesh ended and metal began. Only the pain remained.

The magistrate lifted a hand, silencing them. "Confess"

With the last bit of strength she had she spat "never"

At his nod, the inquisitor stepped forward and removed the screws. She cried out as her ruined fingers slumped against her palm, useless, unnatural. Blood welled from beneath the broken nails, seeping between the cracks of her torn skin.

Ursula gasped awake, her hands shaking as she pressed them against the polished wood of the library table. The weight of the dream clung to her chest, squeezing tight. She had been reading about the witch trials far too much.

The room was still the same: rows of tall shelves filled with old books, the low murmur of students absorbed in their studies, the faint hum of the overhead lights. The only difference was the sweat beading at her brow and the way her breath came fast, as though she had run miles instead of simply reading a book.
She looked down at the aged book beside her laptop, its pages yellowed with time.
Trial Records of 1561: The Lost Witches of Yorkshire. The name was there, staring at her in bold ink.

Ursula Southeil.
Age: 19.
Place of Trial: Knaresborough, Yorkshire.

Her name.
It was her name.

She needed to talk to someone.
Snatching up her bag, she shoved her laptop
and notes inside and hurried towards the
nearest table where a group of students were
deep in discussion. They were all in her history
course, researching their own dissertation
topics.
Charlie was the first to look up, pushing his
glasses up his nose as he eyed her with mild
curiosity. "You okay, Ursula? You look like
you've seen a ghost."

She almost laughed at the irony of that. "I think
I have."
Jodie, a sharp-eyed girl with auburn braids,
raised an eyebrow. "What's going on?"
Ursula exhaled sharply and slid the book onto
the table, flipping it open to the page. "Look at
this."
Their eyes scanned the text, moving over the
details with growing intrigue.
"'Ursula Southeil,'" Charlie read aloud,
frowning. "That's—whoa, that's your name."

"Exactly." Ursula tapped her fingers against the page. "Nineteen years old. Accused of witchcraft. Tortured. Executed." She hesitated before lowering her voice. "And she had a hunch."

Jodie glanced up sharply. "Wait—what?"
"She had a deformity. People called her unnatural. Cursed."

A silence stretched between them.
"That's freaky," Charlie muttered. He drummed his fingers on the table. "Maybe you're, like, related? Distantly?"

"Or maybe," Jodie said, leaning in with a gleam in her eyes, "you're her reincarnation."

Ursula gave a short, humourless laugh. "I don't believe in that."

"Then why do you look like you're about to be sick?"

She had no answer.

The words of the text still burned in her mind. The pain in the dream had felt too real. She had felt the heat of the iron, had smelled her own skin burning.
And the name—her name—was written in history.

Coincidence. It had to be coincidence.

But when she closed her eyes, she could still hear the crank turning.

Chapter 2

The cave was colder than Ursula had expected, the air thick with the damp scent of wet stone and earth. Water dripped steadily from somewhere deep within, the sound echoing off the rough rock walls. She pulled her coat tighter around herself and took another cautious step forward, her boots crunching against the gravelly ground.

It felt strange to be here, standing in the place where Mother Shipton—Ursula Southeil—had supposedly been born. She had read the legends: the deformed girl, feared by the villagers, growing up to be a famed prophetess and healer. Some called her a witch. Others called her wise.

Either way, her name had been etched into history.

And now here she was.

Ursula Southeil. A different one. A modern one.

But the similarities were impossible to ignore.

The name. The hunch. The way people whispered when they thought she couldn't hear. She exhaled, her breath misting in the cold air. She had come here looking for a connection— something to ground the research she was doing for her dissertation. But standing in the cave, surrounded by centuries of history, she suddenly felt out of place.

That was when she saw it.

A small, half-buried wooden box, nestled between two jagged rocks at the cave's edge. Frowning, she crouched down, brushing away the loose soil. The box was old, its wood dark and worn with time, but still intact. Her heart hammered as she pried the lid open, her breath catching when she saw what was inside.

A book.

Its leather cover was cracked with age, the pages yellowed and curled at the edges. Carefully, she lifted it out, dusting away the remnants of earth that clung to its surface.

She flipped it open.

Ursula Southeil – Knaresborough, 1561

Her fingers tightened around the edges of the book.

No.
No way.

The handwriting was uneven, the ink faded but still legible. Beneath the name, the words sent a shiver down her spine.

"They will come for me soon. I hear them coming through the woods. They call me witch. They call me cursed, though I was born with no choice in my shape. I do not fear death, but I fear the pain they will bring before it."

Ursula swallowed hard.

It couldn't be real. Could it?

A voice behind her made her jump.

"Bloody hell, that looks ancient."

She spun around, clutching the book to her chest. Jodie stood at the cave entrance, shaking her hood free of drizzle, eyes wide with curiosity.

Ursula let out a breath, trying to slow her racing heart. "You scared the life out of me."

Jodie grinned, stepping inside. "Charlie said you were coming out here alone. Thought I'd tag along. Didn't expect you to be digging up buried treasure, though." She nodded at the book. "What is that?"

Ursula hesitated, then held it up. "It's a diary. I think it belonged to her."

Jodie frowned. "Mother Shipton?"

Ursula nodded.

Jodie gave a low whistle. "That's insane." She knelt beside her, peering at the open pages. "Can you read it?"

Ursula glanced down, her stomach twisting.

"They brought the iron first, pressed it to my arm. Then came the thumb screws. I heard the bone crack. I felt the pain split me apart. Still, I did not speak the words they wanted. I will not lie."

Ursula's breath hitched.

She had studied the witch trials for weeks now, had read about the instruments of torture used to extract confessions. But reading the words of someone who had endured it was different. Jodie frowned. "The screws?"

Ursula nodded, her voice tight. "Thumb Screws"

Jodie's face scrunched up. "Sounds awful."

"It was," Ursula said. "It was made of iron, designed to hold your thumbs in place, turning the screw at the top until it literally crushed your bones to dust. Then they would move onto the fingers"

Jodie looked horrified. "Jesus."

"They used it to get confessions from people in the middle ages," Ursula continued. "Adulterers. Heretics. Women who wouldn't confess." She swallowed, tracing the words on the page. "Women like her."

Jodie was quiet for a moment, then exhaled, rubbing her arms as if to shake off the chill of the cave. "And you just found this? Sitting here?"

Ursula nodded. "Half-buried, like someone wanted to hide it."

Jodie shook her head. "This is wild. I mean, it's not every day you find a centuries-old diary just lying around. What if no one's seen this before? What if this is—" she gestured at the book, excitement flickering in her eyes, "—like, the missing account of Mother Shipton's trial?"

Ursula's pulse quickened.

That was the thing, wasn't it? The records of her trial were vague. Officially, history only hinted at how she had died. Some said she had escaped execution, living out her days as a prophetess. Others said she had been burned, hanged, or left to rot in a cell.

But here, in her hands, was a firsthand account. A confession that wasn't a confession. A woman's last words before she died.

She turned another page, her breath catching at the next line.

"If you find this, know that I was never what they claimed."

Jodie let out a slow breath. "This is insane." Ursula nodded, barely hearing her.

The ink was darker now, the strokes hurried.

"There are things I wish I had more time to write, but my time is short. They will take me from this cave. I have seen the torches through the trees."

Ursula's hands shook slightly.

"I do not know who will read this, nor when or how, but if you are reading these words, then you are searching for the truth."

She swallowed hard.

Jodie nudged her. "Ursula."

She blinked, looking up.
Jodie pointed to the words at the bottom of the page.

"And if you are searching for the truth... you must beware of the one who still watches."

A gust of wind howled through the cave, sending a chill skittering down Ursula's spine.

Jodie shuddered. "I don't like that."

Ursula closed the diary carefully, her heart hammering.

Neither did she.

Chapter 3

Ursula Southeil – Knaresborough, 1561

The magistrate stepped forward, his boots clicking against the cold stone floor. He bent down, his breath foul with ale and self-importance.

"You are strong," he murmured. "Most confess by now."

Cradling her destroyed hand to her chest, Ursula wanted to spit in his face, but she had no strength left.

He straightened, turning to the crowd. "She bears it well, does she not? A sign of the Devil's endurance, perhaps?"

A murmur of agreement rippled through the gathered villagers. Some nodded solemnly; others watched with curiosity, their eyes flicking from her mangled hand to her face as though she were some specimens to be studied.

"She does not deny it," a voice whispered.

"She speaks no prayers," another muttered.

"She has the mark," someone else added. "The mark of a witch."

She barely had time to catch her breath before they grabbed her, rough hands yanking at the neckline of her dress.

"No—" she gasped, struggling, but there were too many.

The fabric tore, the coarse wool scraping against her raw skin as they pulled it from her shoulders, down past her waist. She kicked, twisted, anything to preserve the last shreds of her dignity, but it was no use.

They stripped her bare. Shaved her body.

A murmur swept through the crowd—low, eager.

Ursula clenched her jaw, the humiliation burning almost as fiercely as the pain. Her body was thin, marked with bruises, the shape of her back curved, her spine twisted. To them, she was anything other than human.

She forced herself to meet their eyes.

Old men, young boys, women with infants at their breasts—all staring.

Judging.

The magistrate cleared his throat, addressing the crowd as though she were a piece of livestock at market. "We shall now seek the Devil's mark."

He stepped aside, allowing another man forward—the pricker.

He was thin, his fingers bony, his eyes dark with cruel delight. In his hand, he held a long iron needle—thin, sharp, gleaming in the candlelight.

A murmur of anticipation rippled through the onlookers.

Ursula swallowed hard.

The pricker knelt beside her, his fingers cold as they gripped her chin, tilting her head this way and that, his eyes scanning her skin as though searching for something hidden beneath it.

She knew what came next.

The magistrate addressed the crowd, his voice carrying over the chamber. "The Devil's mark is the place upon the witch's body where her master drinks of her blood. It is insensible to pain. A true servant of Satan will not bleed."

The pricker smiled.

He raised the needle and drove it into her shoulder.

Ursula gasped, her body jolting as pain lanced through her. Blood welled from the tiny wound, trailing down her bare skin.

A murmur from the crowd.

"She bleeds," someone muttered.

The pricker ignored them. He pressed the needle against her collarbone, sliding it beneath the skin with agonising slowness.

She clenched her jaw so tightly she thought her teeth might crack.

Again, blood dripped from the wound.

Again, the crowd murmured.

"Check her back," someone called.

The pricker's lips curled.

He grabbed her shoulder roughly, forcing her forward. She could not fight him—her arms were weak, her body broken. She shivered as the cold air bit at her exposed skin, as the needle pricked down her spine, searching for the place where her flesh would betray her.

120

He dragged it across her ribs. Down her arm. The back of her knee.

Every time, she bled. Every time, she flinched.

The magistrate frowned, unimpressed.

Until—

"Wait," the pricker said.

He knelt lower, his breath warm against her lower back.

Ursula froze.

She knew what he had seen.

The scar.

It was small, no bigger than a fingernail, a remnant of a childhood fall. A place where the nerves had long since dulled.

The pricker pressed the needle against it.

Ursula did not react.

The crowd went still.

He twisted the needle, deeper, deeper, until it should have drawn blood.

But it did not.

"She does not bleed," the pricker murmured.

A hush fell over them all.

The magistrate's lips curled into a satisfied smile.

"There," he said softly. "Proof."

Ursula tried to speak, to explain, but the words caught in her throat.

Not like it mattered.

They had already decided.

Chapter 4

Ursula sat hunched over the diary, her fingers curled tightly around its worn edges. The dim glow of her desk lamp cast long, flickering shadows over the pages, its light too weak to chase away the weight pressing down on her chest.

She swallowed, her breath coming shallow as she traced the ink with shaking hands.

"The first crack was like thunder in my bones."

Her stomach twisted.

"The screw turned, and I felt the flesh split, the bone yield beneath the pressure. They crushed my fingers one by one. When I did not scream, they turned it again. And again. Until my hand was ruined."

A sob caught in Ursula's throat, sharp and unexpected. She pressed a trembling hand to her lips, as if she could hold back the sound, as if she could stop the raw ache blooming inside her.

But it was already too late.

Tears welled in her eyes, hot and relentless, spilling over as she read on.

"The magistrate smiled as he watched. He told the crowd I was strong. He said strength was the Devil's work. I knew then that no answer I gave would save me."

Ursula's vision blurred. Her hands shook violently as she gripped the book, the words swimming on the yellowed page.

This wasn't just some distant story from history.

This was a woman.

A real woman, flesh and blood, torn apart for nothing.

Ursula let out a choked breath and wiped her eyes furiously, but the tears kept coming, sliding down her cheeks and falling onto the fragile paper.

It wasn't fair.

It wasn't fair that she had been born different and punished for it. That they had called her a witch, that they had looked at her hunch, her shape, and decided she must belong to the Devil.

It wasn't fair that they had broken her body piece by piece and still demanded her confession.

It wasn't fair that she never had a chance.

Ursula turned the page, her vision swimming, her chest rising and falling in ragged gasps.

"Then they stripped me. The hands of men, rough and cruel, tore away my dress. I fought, but my strength was gone. The cold bit at my skin as they pulled me before the crowd, my body bare for all to see."

A sob ripped from her throat, shaking her shoulders.

She clenched the book so tightly her knuckles turned white.

She could see it, feel it, the humiliation, the shame.

Standing there—exposed, vulnerable, her twisted back on display for the entire village to gawk at.

She knew that feeling.

Not in the same way.

Not with her skin bared before a sea of strangers.

But she knew what it was like to be stared at. Judged. To have whispers follow her like shadows, pitying glances that turned to quiet scorn.

She had spent her entire life feeling different, other.

126

But she had never suffered this.

She turned another page, breathless with grief.

"They spoke of the Devil's mark. The place upon my skin where Satan himself had claimed me. They brought forth the pricker, a thin man with cruel hands and a needle longer than my finger."

Ursula hiccupped on a sob, wiping at her wet cheeks. The words blurred; ink smudged by her tears.

But she couldn't stop reading.

"He pierced my skin, dragging the needle along my arms, my ribs, my legs. He pressed it deeper each time, waiting for a place where I would not bleed. The crowd watched, their breaths hushed, their eyes hungry."

Her stomach churned. She clutched at her own arm, as if she could shield herself from the pain described on the page, from the cruelty that had happened centuries ago but still bled into her soul.

The pricker had searched and searched.

And then—

"He found the scar."

Ursula's breath hitched, her fingers gripping the edge of the diary like a lifeline.

"It was small, a mark from childhood. A wound long healed. I did not feel the needle there. I did not bleed."

Her body tensed, the words thick with dread.

She knew what came next.

"The crowd gasped. The pricker smiled. The magistrate nodded."

"There," he said. 'Proof.'"

A strangled noise escaped Ursula's throat, her tears coming harder now, dripping onto the page in thick, wet splashes.

"I did not cry out when they declared me a witch."

"But inside, I knew I was already dead."

Ursula slammed the book shut, clutching it to her chest as sobs wracked her body.

She couldn't take it anymore.

The cruelty. The absolute, pointless cruelty.

She rocked slightly in her chair, pressing the diary against her as if she could absorb the pain, as if she could somehow take it from the past and make it her own so that she had suffered instead—so that she had borne it, instead of the girl whose name she shared.

She cried for her.

For what they had done.

For the broken fingers. The bared skin. The needle pressing into her back as strangers waited for her to fail.

She cried because history had forgotten her.

Because Ursula Southeil, the real one, had been a person, not just a myth, not just some old woman in folktales.

And this was the first time—maybe in centuries—that someone had truly listened to her words.

The tears didn't stop for a long time.

When she finally pulled herself together, when the sobs had faded to shaky breaths and her chest ached from the weight of it all, she looked at her phone.

A message from Jodie.

You alright? You left in a hurry.

Her fingers hovered over the screen. The words wouldn't come.

But she couldn't keep this to herself.

With a deep breath, she typed back.

I found something.

A pause. Then—

Come over. Tell me everything.

Ursula wiped her eyes with the back of her sleeve. Her fingers still shook as she reached for the diary again, her heart pounding in her ribs.

She didn't know what she was going to say.

But she knew one thing for certain.

She would make sure this Ursula Southeil wasn't forgotten again.

Chapter 5

Ursula Southeil – Knaresborough, 1561

The stone floor was wet beneath her cheek, slick with filth and the blood of those who had come before her. Her breath rattled in her lungs, every gasp a struggle against the agony wrapping her body like chains.

The dungeon reeked of rot and despair, the air thick with damp, mould creeping up the walls like fingers. It was a place without time. Without light. Without mercy.

Heavy footsteps echoed through the chamber, deliberate and slow.

The magistrate knelt beside her, his fingers gripping her chin, forcing her to look up. His breath was hot with ale, his gaze filled with something close to pity—but not quite.

"You have endured much, Ursula Southeil," he murmured, tilting his head as if she were a puzzle he could not solve.

She said nothing. Her jaw ached too much to move, her body broken and raw from their last round of torment.

He exhaled through his nose, disappointed. "Most confess by now."

Ursula let out a slow breath, her ribs burning. "Then they were fools."

The magistrate's lips curled. "No, my dear. They were wise."

His fingers left her chin, and he stood, brushing the dust from his robes. "You have been tested by fire and by steel. You have bled. You have suffered." He turned slightly, glancing toward the shadows where the gaoler stood waiting. "Yet still, you refuse to confess."

Ursula swallowed, tasting blood on her tongue. "Because I am no witch."

The magistrate gave her a look almost akin to amusement.

"It is not the truth that matters, girl. It is the words you speak." He stepped aside, gesturing toward something in the corner of the chamber. "And you will speak to them soon."

The gaoler moved forward, dragging something heavy across the ground.

Ursula's stomach twisted as the thing emerged into the dim torchlight.

The boot.

She had heard the screams of others who had worn it before.

A contraption of thick iron, its shape crude, its purpose simple: destruction.

It was fitted around the lower leg, clamping the flesh tight within its cold embrace. Then came the wedges—thick wooden blocks driven between boot and bone, each strike of the mallet forcing them deeper.

Until the leg cracked like dry kindling.

Until there was nothing left to break.

A thin smile tugged at the magistrate's lips. "You are strong, Ursula. But even stone will shatter under enough pressure."

The gaoler seized her arms, dragging her forward.

Her limbs were weak, unresponsive, but she still tried to struggle. It was instinct—one last act of defiance, even as her body betrayed her.

The boot was fitted to her right leg first, its iron plates locking into place. Her breath came quick and shallow as the gaoler fastened the straps, binding her limb in a steel embrace.

The wedges were brought forth, placed at the front of the boot, pressing against her shin.

The gaoler took up the mallet.

Ursula clenched her fists, nails biting into her palms.

The first blow fell.

A sharp burst of pressure. Pain blossomed, but not unbearable. Not yet.

The magistrate watched her closely, waiting.

The second blow.

The wedge pressed deeper, cutting into the muscle, pinning the flesh against the cold iron.

Ursula gritted her teeth. She would not give them the satisfaction.

The third blow.

Something shifted within her leg—something unnatural.

The pain flared hot and bright, radiating through her body like fire. A strangled sound slipped from her lips before she could swallow it.

The magistrate's smile widened. "There it is."

The fourth blow.

A sharp, wet crack.

Ursula screamed.

White-hot agony exploded through her, searing and relentless. Her body convulsed, her vision darkening at the edges. The pressure inside her leg was unbearable—the bone forced inward, splintering beneath the wedge.

The fifth blow.

Her leg gave way entirely.

The sound of it was worse than the pain. A sickening crunch, followed by the sensation of something shifting where it should not shift.

Ursula barely registered the magistrate crouching beside her again, his voice low, smooth. "Confess, child."

She shook her head, teeth clenched so tightly her jaw ached. Tears streaked her cheeks, her breath coming in ragged gasps.

He sighed. "Then we continue."

The boot was fitted to her left leg.

Her mind screamed no, no, no—but her voice was gone, lost somewhere in the fog of pain.

The mallet rose.

The first blow fell.

She did not remember much after that.

Only the pain.

Only the darkness.

Chapter 6

Ursula laughed as Jodie nudged her playfully, nearly causing her to spill her drink. The pub was lively tonight, filled with the murmur of conversation, the clinking of glasses, and the occasional burst of laughter from the tables around them. The scent of spilled ale and fried food lingered in the air, mixing with the warmth of bodies packed close together.

"You should've seen your face in that cave," Jodie teased, stirring the ice in her glass. "You looked like you'd found the Ark of the Covenant or something."

Ursula rolled her eyes, but she couldn't help but grin. "To be fair, I did find something pretty bloody important."

"Still wild," Charlie added, leaning forward on his elbows. "A firsthand account of a witch trial? That's like dissertation gold."

"Exactly." Ursula took a sip of her drink, letting the warmth settle in her stomach. "I've been thinking about how to frame it. The diary is clearly a personal account of the trial, but I need to put it in context. I can't just write 'Look, I found a secret book in a cave, give me a first-class degree.'"

Jodie smirked. "Why not? Sounds like a solid thesis to me."

Charlie chuckled. "You still meeting with Dr. Loughton tomorrow?"

Ursula nodded, drumming her fingers against the side of her glass. "Yeah. I need his advice. There are so many angles I could take with this, but I don't want to just rehash what's already been done."

Jodie tilted her head. "Like what?"

"Well," Ursula began, leaning back, "I could look at the legal side—how witch trials fit into early modern law, how evidence was manipulated, how confession was forced through torture."

Charlie winced. "That'd be grim."

"Yeah, but it's important," Ursula said. "People forget how systematic it was. They think witch trials were just random superstitions, but they weren't. They were methodical. Everything was done in steps—accusation, interrogation, torture, confession. And once you confessed, that was it. Game over."

Jodie exhaled. "Jesus. When you put it like that..."

Ursula nodded. "Or I could focus on gender. How it was mostly women accused, and how it was really about control. A woman who lived alone? Suspicious. A woman who knew medicine? Witch. A woman who spoke her mind? Definitely in league with the Devil."

Jodie snorted. "Sounds like my aunt when she's had too much wine."

Charlie grinned. "Or the tabloids every time a woman does literally anything."

Ursula smirked. "Exactly." She tapped her fingers on the table. "Or I could approach it from a personal angle. Use the diary as a case study—examine her story and how it fits into the larger picture."

Jodie pointed her drink at her. "That one. That's the winner. Because this isn't just any case— you've got her own words. That's rare, right?"

Ursula nodded. "Very rare. Most of what we have about accused witches is from court records written by the accusers. We never get to hear their voices. But with this diary... it's her side of the story."

Charlie leaned back, nodding thoughtfully. "That's powerful."

Ursula smiled, feeling a thrill of excitement. "Yeah. It is."

She glanced at her watch and groaned. "Speaking of which, I should probably get home. I have to be coherent for my meeting with Dr. Loughton tomorrow."

Jodie grinned. "Oh yeah, wouldn't want to explain centuries of injustice while hungover."

Charlie laughed. "Good luck with the professor. Let us know what he says."

Ursula drained the rest of her drink and grabbed her coat, feeling a strange sense of anticipation. She had been drowning in the past for weeks, lost in old records and the weight of what she had read. But for the first time, it felt like she had a direction.

A purpose.

Dr. Loughton's office was as cluttered as ever, books stacked precariously on every available surface, yellowed maps pinned to the walls, a faded globe with a crack running through the Atlantic. The scent of old paper filled the air, mingling with the faint aroma of black coffee.

Ursula sat across from his desk, her notebook balanced on her lap. Dr. Loughton was flipping through the papers she had sent him earlier, his brow furrowed in concentration. He was an older man, with greying hair and a sharp, analytical gaze that always made students sit up straighter.

After a long silence, he leaned back and steepled his fingers. "This," he said, "is incredibly interesting."

Ursula's heart kicked up a beat. "You think so?"

He nodded. "If this diary is legitimate—and I'll want to verify that, of course—then this is one of the most significant primary sources on English witch trials we've seen in decades."

A thrill ran through her. "I thought so too."

Dr. Loughton tapped a finger against the desk. "Now, tell me, Ursula—what do you want to say with this?"

She hesitated, then took a deep breath. "I want to bring her story to life. To show that she wasn't just a name in a trial record, but a person. To show how these trials weren't just about superstition—they were about fear, power, and control."

Dr. Loughton smiled slightly. "Good. That's exactly the right approach. But you'll need to be meticulous. If you're making the claim that this is an authentic firsthand account, you'll need to prove it. Cross-referencing trial records, handwriting analysis, paper dating—"

"I know," Ursula said quickly. "I've already started gathering sources to back it up."

"Excellent." He leaned forward. "You've got something special here, Ursula. But be careful. History is written by the victor and when it is rewritten, people don't always like what they see."

Ursula frowned. "What do you mean?"

Dr. Loughton gave her a knowing look. "Witch trials weren't just about witches. They were about who gets to control the narrative. And even centuries later, people are invested in keeping certain versions of history intact."

A chill prickled at the back of her neck.

She nodded slowly. "I'll be careful."

Dr. Loughton studied her for a moment, then nodded. "Then you have my support. I'll guide you through the process, help you get the right sources, and if we can verify the diary—" he smiled, "—you might just change how we understand this period of history."

Ursula exhaled, a slow, determined smile forming.

She had started this out of curiosity, a strange coincidence of names. But now?

Now, she was doing it for her.

For the Ursula Southeil who had been tortured and silenced.

For the women who had been erased from history.

And no matter what she found next, she wasn't going to stop.

Chapter 7

Ursula Southeil – Knaresborough, 1561

She had not known that pain could reach this depth—that it could linger, coiling through her bones like a living thing, pressing against the very edges of her soul.

Her body had long since stopped feeling like her own. The fingers that had been crushed in the thumbscrews were swollen, misshapen, their broken bones shifting beneath her skin with every movement. Her legs—her legs—were worse. The boots had shattered them. She knew it. Every attempt to move sent a sickening wave of pain through her, as though her limbs no longer belonged to her but to the inquisitor's tools.

And yet, they still wanted more.

The magistrate's voice drifted through the haze, calm and measured, as if he were discussing the weather. "Still, she does not confess."

A murmur from the gathered men, their dark robes shifting in the flickering torchlight.

"She endures beyond reason," one of them muttered.

"She is stubborn," another corrected.

"She is a witch," the magistrate said firmly.

Ursula wanted to laugh. The sound almost escaped her lips, but all that came out was a dry, broken wheeze.

What was there left to break?

She should have been dead already. Should have slipped into the cold embrace of the grave and been free of them, of their tools, of their eager, greedy eyes watching as she suffered.

But they would not let her die yet.

Not until she spoke the words they wanted.

The chains around her wrists clanked as they dragged her forward, her body limp in their grasp. She could no longer stand, not with her ruined legs, but the inquisitor hauled her up like a rag doll, their fingers digging into her raw, bruised flesh.

And then she saw it.

The rack.

A crude thing—wooden, simple, its surface darkened with sweat and blood. The rollers at either end gleamed in the torchlight, the ropes hanging slack, waiting to be pulled taut.

Her stomach twisted.

She had heard of the rack before. Had heard the stories.

Limbs wrenched from sockets. Tendons snapping like taut strings. Bones stretched until they split apart, muscle tearing under the strain.

It was the kind of pain that ruined a body, leaving it less than human.

The magistrate stepped closer. "This, dear child, will be the end of your resistance. You see, we do not require your words anymore. Your body will confess for you."

Ursula lifted her head just enough to meet his eyes. "You are the ones who belong to the Devil."

A flicker of irritation crossed his face. "Put her on it."

The inquisitor obeyed.

She felt herself lifted, her limbs placed carefully as if she were a piece of meat to be trussed. Her wrists were fastened to the ropes, her ankles secured in place.

A deep breath.

A second of silence.

And then the first turn of the rollers.

Pain shot through her shoulders as the ropes tightened, pulling her arms upward, forcing her body into unnatural tension.

Another turn.

The stretch deepened. Her joints groaned under the pressure.

Another turn.

Her shoulders popped, the sockets dislocating. Fire lanced through her, spreading from her back to her chest, stealing her breath.

She cried out.

The men murmured in approval.

Another turn.

Her legs—already ruined from the boots—were forced straight, her battered muscles screaming in protest as the bones beneath them shifted.

She felt something in her hip tear.

A deep, sickening snap followed.

She screamed, her voice raw and ragged, the agony overwhelming everything else.

The magistrate watched. The inquisitor tightened the ropes.

Still, she did not confess.

They left her there, stretched to her very limits, her breath coming in shallow gasps. Every movement sent fresh waves of pain through her. Her vision darkened at the edges, her consciousness slipping.

Then the rack was loosened.

Her body collapsed inward, her limbs falling uselessly at her sides, her shoulders burning, her legs twitching with each jagged nerve impulse.

She wanted to beg for death.

But they were not finished with her yet.

The scavenger's daughter was waiting.

The device was smaller than the rack but no less cruel. A metal frame designed to crush instead of stretch.

She was barely aware of them moving her—of her arms being pulled inward, of her legs folding until she was curled into herself like a discarded thing.

The frame pressed around her, a cold iron embrace.

Then it began to close.

Pain, sharp and immediate, as her broken limbs were forced together, bones shifting, muscles bruising against themselves.

Her ribs compressed, the breath stolen from her lungs.

Her knees crushed against her chest, her broken legs grinding, the pressure unbearable.

Her spine twisted, her already curved back screaming in protest.

It felt as if her entire body was imploding, folding in on itself like a dying star.

Her mind swam, her vision flickering.

Somewhere in the distance, she heard the magistrate's voice.

"Confess, and it ends."

Her lips parted. A sound escaped.

A whimper. A plea.

Not for mercy.

Not for freedom.

But for death.

She could not take more. Her body could not endure more.

The device tightened.

Her ribs creaked.

Her vision went black.

And at last—she let go.

Chapter 8

The diary lay open before Ursula, the pages trembling beneath her hands. Her stomach twisted with every word, every brutal description of pain, every method of torture that had been used to break the other Ursula Southeil.

But she hadn't broken.

Not until the very end.

Ursula wiped a hand across her face, realising only then that she was crying again. It was unbearable, the weight of it. The crushing boots, the rack, the scavenger's daughter. The way they had reduced a woman—a living, breathing person—into something less than human.

And for what?

Because she was different. Because she scared them.

She exhaled shakily and pushed the book away, rubbing her temples. The air in her flat felt heavy, suffocating. She needed a break, some kind of distraction, anything to pull herself away from what she had just read.

She turned to her laptop, fingers hesitating over the keyboard before she typed into the search bar:

Ursula Southeil (Mother Shipton) witch trial records.

A list of articles popped up, ranging from serious historical essays to wild conspiracy theories. She clicked on a magazine article from the BBC Countryfile, scanning the page.

Born in 1488, Ursula Southeil—later known as Mother Shipton—was a reputed prophetess who allegedly foresaw modern technology centuries before it was invented. Among her supposed predictions were:
• The invention of cars, trains, and planes
• Telegraphy and wireless communication
• The rise of iron ships replacing wooden vessels

• A great war spanning the world

Ursula's eyebrows shot up. She had expected the usual witch trial accusations—cursing livestock, consorting with demons, that sort of thing. But this?

This was something else.

Her gaze flickered to the passage that referenced Mother Shipton's home.

From a cave near Knaresborough, her arrival into the world was surrounded by legend. The cave is home to the so-called 'petrifying well,' where objects left in the water turn to stone.

Ursula frowned.

That had to be an exaggeration. Surely it was just mineral deposits or something. She opened a new tab and searched:

How does the Petrifying Well work?

The explanation was immediate.

"The well's unique properties are caused by high levels of dissolved minerals in the water. Over time, as water evaporates, minerals build up around objects, creating a stone-like coating. It is the same natural process that forms stalactites in caves."

Ursula let out a breath. So that was it. Nothing magical, nothing supernatural—just science.

The cave where Mother Shipton had been from wasn't cursed. It wasn't proof of demonic influence. It was just a geological phenomenon that people in the 1500s couldn't explain.

And yet...

Her stomach twisted as she reread the part about the prophecies.

How had a woman in the sixteenth century predicted things like trains and planes?

Ursula swallowed.

160

Some of it could be explained, right? Maybe she had observed trends in technology, the same way Leonardo da Vinci had sketched designs for flying machines. Maybe the predictions were just stories exaggerated over time.

But still.

Something inside her refused to let it go.

She clicked on another article, scanning the transcribed verses of Mother Shipton's supposed prophecies.

"Carriages without horses shall go,
And accidents fill the world with woe.
Around the world thoughts shall fly
In the twinkling of an eye."

Cars. Telegraphy.

"Under water, men shall walk,
Shall ride, shall sleep, shall talk."

Submarines.

"Iron in the water shall float,
As easy as a wooden boat."

Modern ships.

Ursula's hands grew clammy. These weren't
vague, Nostradamus-style riddles that could
mean anything. They were specific. Too specific.

But how?

How had a woman in the 1500s, a woman
accused of witchcraft, of dealing with the Devil
foreseen a world that wouldn't exist for
hundreds of years?

Ursula sat back in her chair, heart pounding.

There had to be an explanation.

Maybe the prophecies had been fabricated long
after her death, written by later writers to make
her seem more mystical than she really was.
Maybe they had been rewritten so many times
that they had lost their original meaning.

But a nagging voice in the back of her mind whispered, what if they weren't?

What if Ursula Southeil had seen something real?

She looked back at the diary, sitting on her desk, its aged pages fluttering slightly in the draft from the window.

A woman who had been tortured for being different.

A woman who had suffered beyond what a human body should have been able to endure.

A woman who had known things.

Ursula took a deep breath.

She had set out to study history—to understand the past through cold, hard facts. But the more she uncovered, the more she realised...

Not everything could be explained.

Chapter 9

Ursula Southeil – Knaresborough, 1561

Darkness had become her only companion.

She had lost track of time, the hours bleeding into each other like ink spreading through water. The damp, stinking cell was no longer cold—she had passed the point of feeling it. The stone walls pressed in, their silence mocking her suffering.

The metal collar around her neck was tight, its rusted edges digging into her skin, keeping her fixed against the wall like an animal in a butcher's pen. Her limbs, broken and battered, were useless. The pain was constant, her body beyond exhaustion.

And yet, in the depths of her agony, there was something else.

Relief.

They would kill her soon.

The thought did not frighten her. It did not fill her with dread or despair. It filled her with something close to peace.

The torture was over. There was nothing left to break, nothing left to hang.

They would take her to their trial—though there would be no justice, only judgment. They would speak their accusations, their voices thick with lies. And then they would do what they had always planned to do.

They would soon hang her.

And she would finally be free.

The iron collar was unfastened with a sharp clang, and rough hands seized her arms, dragging her forward. She barely felt it. Her feet scraped across the filthy floor as she was hauled from her cell, through the narrow stone passageways of the gaol, up into the world above.

The trial chamber was filled with people—too many people. The heat of their bodies, the murmur of their voices, the weight of their eyes on her, watching, waiting, judging.

She was thrown to the floor before the magistrate.

The man who had ordered her broken.

The man who now sat before her, dressed in his fine robes, his lips curled in satisfaction as he looked upon the ruin of her.

Ursula did not kneel. Could not kneel. She remained where they had thrown her, her arms limp at her sides, her legs twisted unnaturally.

The crowd whispered.

She heard her name. Heard the word witch like the hiss of a snake through the chamber.

She smiled.

They thought this was punishment. They thought this was victory.

They did not realise that they had lost the moment they had failed to break her.

The magistrate stood. His voice rang out, solemn and authoritative.

"Ursula Southeil, you stand accused of witchcraft, consorting with the Devil, and the murder of Thomas Weaver, the town baker, through witchcraft."

Ursula let out a slow breath.

Ah. So they had decided to burn her after all.

The baker had been an old man, weak in the chest. But it did not matter. He was dead, and they needed a death to justify the stake and their cruelty.

The magistrate continued, his voice smooth with the false dignity of justice. "You were seen, arriving from the depths of hell. You murdered the baker with your witchcraft and watched as he collapsed and died. You bear the mark of the Devil upon your back. You are a WITCH"

Ursula chuckled.

It was a thin, broken sound, barely more than a whisper. But it carried through the chamber, silencing the crowd.

The magistrate's mouth twisted in distaste. "Do you laugh at your own damnation?"

She lifted her head, meeting his gaze.

"You call this damnation?" she rasped. "You think I fear death?"

A murmur ran through the room.

The magistrate's nostrils flared. "You do not deny the charges?"

Ursula smiled, the taste of blood thick on her tongue. "I deny nothing. I confess nothing." She shifted, the pain in her ribs stabbing through her. "But it doesn't matter, does it? You decided my fate long before this day."

The magistrate narrowed his eyes.

She had beaten him.
Not by escaping, not by winning her freedom, but by refusing to fear what was coming.

He lifted the sentencing scroll. "You are found guilty of witchcraft and murder."

The words did not sting.

He continued.

"You shall be taken to the town square at first light. As you have killed an innocent with your witchcraft, you will be tied to the stake, and you will burn until your soul is cleansed from this evil."

The crowd exhaled as one—some in satisfaction, some in unease.

Ursula closed her eyes.

Burning.

It would be agony. A death of fire and smoke, of lungs turning to embers, of flesh curling away from the bone.

But it would be an ending.

A release from the hands that had shattered her. From the ropes, the chains, the iron.

And in the flames, she would be free.

She opened her eyes and fixed the magistrate with the last defiance she had left.

"You may burn my body," she said, voice raw but steady. "But you will never burn the truth."

The magistrate's jaw tightened.

And Ursula Southeil smiled as they dragged her away, eager for the moment when the fire would finally take her.

Chapter 10

Ursula Southeil – Knaresborough, 1561

The cell is damp, the stone weeping as though it, too, dreads what is to come. The only light comes from a small, barred window high above me. I can see the sky and the rain falling. I watched the drops slide down the wall like tears.

The guards give me water and hard bread, enough to give me the strength so I burn properly, but not enough to fight back. I chew slowly, forcing myself to eat. Hunger does not concern them. Only the spectacle matters—the crowd must see me strong enough to scream.

I hear them outside, their talking, their slurs, their prayers. Some call me a monster. Others say nothing, those are the ones who trouble me most. Silence, after all, is not the absence of belief but the confirmation of it.

One guard lingers when he brings my food. I see it in his eyes—the smallest flicker of doubt. He doesn't speak but doubt needs no voice. It is in the way his hands shake when he passes me the cup, the way he doesn't look away as the others do.

I take a risk. When he returns and whisper:

"When you dream, do you dream of fire?"

He says nothing. But I see the answer in his face.

I do not know his name, only that he is younger than the others. He does not spit at me, does not jeer unlike the others as they pass my cell at night, emboldened by the safety of their numbers.

The others call me a witch with sharp, laughing tongues. But he does not. Not once.

I watch him as he leaves. His shoulders are rigid, but his steps are slow, as though something weighs on him. Perhaps guilt. Perhaps something deeper.

The priest came today. He brought the magistrate. They asked me if I would repent, if I would beg for God's mercy. I told them mercy is not theirs to give.

They did not like that.

They spat on me. They are afraid I will cast some spell, speak some curse before the flames take me.

They do not understand. My power has never been in words spoken aloud.

It is in words that remain.

I clutch my diary in the darkness, pressing my fingers to the ink. I will not let them take everything from me.

They have built the pyre. I hear them outside, hammering the wooden beams into place. Some villagers work in silence, but others speak as they labour, their voices full of righteousness.

They speak of cleansing. Of justice. Of God's will.

I wonder if they will look into my eyes when they set the fire.

The guard came again tonight. He placed the bread on the floor and hesitated. I watched him shift on his feet before he finally spoke, his voice barely more than breath.

"They say you consort with demons."

I smiled then, though my lips were dry and cracked.

"Do I look like I have had such company?"

He frowned but said no more.

I do not know if he believes I am innocent. I do not think it matters. What matters is that he is listening.

The priest arrived for the final time.

He stood outside my cell, watching me. His hands, always folded over his stomach like a man deep in thought, clenched and unclenched in slow, measured movements.

"You can still be saved," he said. "Confess," he urged. "Ask for His mercy. Renounce the Devil, and perhaps we will spare your soul."

I tilted my head. "Will you spare my body?"

His jaw tightened. He knew the answer as well as I did. He did not speak again.

I am to burn at first light.

The sky is still dark when they come for me. I hear the murmurs of the waking village, the eager anticipation of the crowd.

The guard enters first, torch in hand, his face paler than before. He does not look at me as he unties the metal collar. The others are close behind him, ready to hurt me if I resist.

Like I could resist the inevitable.

But just before we leave, I lean into him and press the diary into his hand.

His breath catches. His eyes widen.

"Where?" he whispers.

"The cave beneath Black Hollow Hill," I say.

A long silence. Then a nod.

He tucks the pages beneath his cloak.

The door opens.

The sky is lighter now, streaked with the first hints of dawn. I'm dragged forward against the cold stone, my body aching.

I know he will keep his promise. I know my words will rest beneath the earth, safe from the fire.

I will burn.

But my truth will not.

Chapter 11

Ursula sat at her desk, fingers hovering over the keyboard. The glow from her laptop screen illuminated the clutter of papers and books surrounding her, the coffee cup beside her long since cold.

She had typed the title at least three times already, each attempt feeling heavier than the last.

"The Trial of Ursula Southeil: Witchcraft, Justice, and the Breaking of Women."

With a deep breath, she forced herself to focus. This was the final stretch. Once she finished this dissertation, she could finally move on.

No more nightmares of cracking bones and burning flesh. No more reading about thumbscrews and boots and the rack.

Just history. Cold, hard history.

She started typing.

"The English witch trials were not merely a product of superstition but a systematic process of persecution, often targeting those who did not conform to societal norms. Ursula Southeil's trial in 1561 was a prime example of this, demonstrating how women—particularly those who were different—were not only accused of witchcraft but subjected to cruel and methodical torture until they confessed to crimes they did not commit..."

The words flowed faster than she expected. It was as though the weeks of research, of horror, of sleepless nights spent reading that cursed diary were finally taking shape.

She could make sense of it now.

But that didn't mean she felt okay.

Later that evening, she sat at a booth in her usual pub, stirring her drink absentmindedly as Jodie and Charlie argued over something ridiculous.

"I'm just saying," Charlie insisted, waving his hands for emphasis, "if we lived in the Middle Ages, I'd absolutely be a knight."

Jodie snorted. "You? A knight? You can't even win at pub trivia, mate."

Charlie groaned. "That was one time."

"Three times," Ursula muttered, smirking as she took a sip of her drink.

Charlie shot her an exasperated look. "What?"

"Just stating facts."

Jodie grinned. "She's got you there."

Ursula smiled, warmth creeping back into her chest. It felt normal to be here, with them, talking about pointless things instead of reading about bones breaking beneath iron screws.

But the weight in her chest hadn't fully lifted.

Jodie must have noticed, because she nudged her arm. "You alright? You seem... I dunno, quieter than usual."

Ursula hesitated.

"I guess I'm just relieved to be done with it," she admitted. "The dissertation. The research. It was... a lot."

Jodie and Charlie exchanged glances.

Charlie leaned forward. "So, the diary... you never said. What did you do with it?"

Ursula exhaled. "I gave it to Dr. Loughton. He's looking into verifying its authenticity."

Jodie raised an eyebrow. "And you're just... done with it?"

Ursula hesitated. "I want to be."

Silence hung between them for a moment before she sighed, rubbing her temples. "Look, I know it's history. I know it happened centuries ago. But reading that diary, seeing what she went through… It didn't feel like history. It felt real."

Jodie reached for her drink, thoughtful. "Maybe because, in a way, it is. I mean, sure, we don't burn witches anymore—"

"Debatable," Charlie muttered. "Have you seen social media?"

Jodie rolled her eyes. "people are still treated like crap for stepping out of line. It's just changed forms."

Ursula nodded slowly. "Yeah. That's what I wrote about. The way the trials weren't just about witches. They were about control. Fear of woman who didn't fit."

Charlie let out a low whistle. "Heavy stuff."

"You have no idea."

Jodie sipped her drink. "So, what now?"

Ursula thought about it. About the sleepless nights, the diary filled with pain, the way she had felt trapped in the past.

And then she thought about this sitting here, with her friends, in a world where she was free to drink, to laugh, to exist.

"I move on," she said finally. "I finish my dissertation, I get my degree, and I put this all behind me."

Charlie raised his glass. "To that, I'll drink."

Jodie clinked her glass against his, then against Ursula's. "To moving on."

Ursula smiled.
And, for the first time in weeks, she actually meant it.

Chapter 12

The night air was crisp as Ursula left the pub, her breath misting in the cold. She pulled her jacket tighter around herself, tucking her hands into the pockets as she made her way through the quiet streets.

The laughter and warmth of the evening still lingered in her mind, but an unease crept over her as she walked. Maybe it was the exhaustion of weeks of research, or maybe it was just the lingering weight of everything.

She exhaled and shook her head. It's over. It's done. Move on.

A sudden flash lit up the sky.

Ursula flinched, glancing up. Dark clouds churned overhead, thick and restless, but there was no thunder—just the strange, erratic flicker of light, almost like heat lightning but sharper, more jagged.

Another flash.

This time, closer.

Her heart thumped faster.

She quickened her pace, her boots echoing against the pavement. Just get home. Get inside.

Another crack of light, this one blinding.

Ursula stumbled back, shielding her eyes.

It was coming from in front of her now—not the sky, but the street itself.

A strange, pulsing glow, as if the air itself was tearing open.

Her breath caught in her throat.

And then,

The world exploded in white.

The ground beneath her was suddenly dirt. The cold of the pavement was gone. The smell of the city had vanished, replaced by the thick, pungent scent of damp earth and wood smoke.

Ursula gasped, her stomach lurching, her head spinning and aching.

What?

Where?

The dim glow of firelight flickered around her. Stone buildings loomed in the mist; thatched roofs dark with rain. The air was thick with the scent of candles, unwashed bodies, something burning in the distance.

It was wrong.

All of it was wrong.

She staggered forward, heart pounding wildly, her boots kicking up mud. Mud.

She hadn't been on a muddy street. She had been in the city. It had been winter. It had been...

A scream cut through the night.

Ursula spun, her breath catching as a figure stepped from the shadows.

A man.

His clothes were rough, filthy with flour and soot. His face was twisted in pure horror, his hands shaking as he pointed directly at her.

His mouth opened, and the word that came out sent ice through her veins.

"Witch!"

The world tilted beneath her.

No.

No, no, no, no, no.

This couldn't be happening. This wasn't real.

The man stumbled back, eyes wide with fear. His lips trembled as he choked out the words again, louder, shaking.

"She—she comes from the depths of hell!"

His body suddenly seized, his arms jerking unnaturally. He gasped, his breath rattling, then collapsed to the ground, his limbs twitching once before going still.

Dead.

The man was dead.

Ursula's blood froze.

The whispers started immediately.

Dark figures moved in the shadows, torches illuminating their faces. Eyes turned toward her, wide with terror.

The murmurs rose—low, urgent, dangerous.

"She came in the storm."

"She killed the baker."

"She stands where he fell."

"She is marked!"

And then, "Burn the witch!"

Ursula took a shaking step backward.

She knew those words. She had read them in the diary.

She had written about them in her dissertation.

And now

Now they were for her.

A wave of sheer, blinding panic surged through her, and she did the only thing she could.

She ran to the only place she knew.

The cave.

The Shadow Man

Chapter 1

There was nothing before this: no memories, images, or sounds—just the absence of something.

A blank space in her mind where something should have been. She didn't know where she had come from but something was definitely missing.

Before this cold.

Before this silence.

Before this cage.

A flicker, a feeling so faint it almost wasn't there.

Warmth.

Not heat or fire—just warmth and comfort.

A familiar and safe presence wrapped around her like a soft embrace. Unbidden, the world formed in her mind like a whisper from another life.

190

She could almost hear it—the distant hum of voices. She could feel the hands running through her hair. A voice murmuring with words of comfort and safety.

A home.

A life.

Hadn't she had one?

Hadn't she existed somewhere before now?

The memory was blurred, slipping through her grasp like water. The warmth, the voices, the golden glow slowly fading.

She gasped, her body trembling, her fingers curling into weak fists as the last remnants of the memory vanished.

She reached for it, desperate, aching—but it was gone.

Damp air clung to her skin, dragging her back into now.

Everything was gone.

Had it even been real? Was it a memory or just a dream of what she longed for? Or had she only imagined it—a trick of her mind, trying to protect her from the truth?

Because this was reality, this was her here and now. Damp, rotten wood beneath her bare skin, bars stretching so high she couldn't see the top. She reached for one, her fingers shaking as they brushed against the rough grain, the solid timber. This was real. This was unbreakable.

Panic surged through her chest, cold and sharp, constricting her ribs like a vice. Where was she? Why couldn't she remember?

She turned, scanning the dim, hazy space beyond the bars: darkness, no sky, no windows. Just shadows shifting in the silence, creeping along the damp ground like living things.

The air was thick with the scent of mildew, earth, and something metallic.

Her stomach twisted; her throat tightened.
Something was wrong. Something was very,
very wrong. She tried to speak, to whisper even
a single word— But no sound came.

Nothing.

Like her voice had been stolen, or she never had
one.

Her breath hitched, and her chest rose and fell
too fast. She gripped the cage bars tighter, her
heartbeat a thudding drumbeat in the silence.
There had been something before this.

A home. A voice. A name.

She knew it.

She knew it.

Didn't she?

Her pulse pounded against her ribs. The
shadows seemed to stretch closer, pressing
against the edges of her vision. She was alone,

with nothing but the silence and the bars that reached too high to climb.

And somewhere in her mind, the memory of warm hands and the golden light faded into nothing like it had never been there at all.

Chapter 2

Her cries were relentless, raw, desperate, clawing at the stale air of the dimly lit room.

She sobbed until her chest ached, until her breath came in ragged gasps, until the walls seemed to close in around her. The sound of her fear was the only thing that existed, bouncing off the cracked wallpaper, swallowed by the silence beyond the door.

She gripped the wooden cage bars, her small fingers trembling against the splintering surface. The wood was rough, worn, and thick, too thick for her to break, no matter how hard she pushed or pulled.

She had tried rocking back and forth to no avail.

She had slammed her fists against it until her knuckles turned red and had clawed at the corners of the cage until her nails bent backwards, the skin beneath them torn, bleeding and throbbing.

Nothing gave.

She was trapped.

A fresh sob wracked her body, shaking her shoulders as she curled into herself. The threadbare mattress beneath her was cold and so thin she could feel the wooden planks sticky and damp in places. It smelled musty, the scent of old wood and something sour clinging to the air.

A slow drip echoed from somewhere in the shadows, rhythmic, endless, a sound she had listened to for what felt like days. Or hours. She didn't know anymore.

Drip, drip, drip.

How long had she been here?
It made her wonder who else had been in here before her.

What they had done to be selected.

Her stomach was empty, aching with a dull, gnawing hunger. Her throat burned from screaming, from crying, from whispering for help into the silence. Her limbs were stiff, her body sore from lying on the thin mattress, shifting restlessly within the cramped space of her prison.

No one had come.

No one had answered her cries.
She let out another broken sob, shaking the bars with weak, frantic hands. She wasn't meant to be here. Someone had to be looking for her. Someone had to know she was gone. She couldn't remember who that should be, but everyone had someone, didn't they?

Didn't they?

She tried again, her voice cracking, rising into the darkness. A long, drawn-out wail. A plea. A scream.

The sound of her own panic filled her ears, but it didn't break through the walls.

She slammed her palm against the bars, her breath shuddering. Her body trembled from exhaustion, but she couldn't stop.

Another scream. Louder. Then—footsteps.

She froze.

Her breath caught in her throat, her fingers stiffening against the bars. The sound was faint but deliberate, the slow creak of wood beneath heavy footsteps. Someone was outside the door.

She swallowed a whimper, pressing herself against the far side of the cage. Her heart pounded, the silence between each step stretching into unbearable eternity.

The footsteps stopped. A pause.

The door handle began to slowly turn.

Her breath hitched as she shrank back, her body pressing so hard against the bars that they dug into her skin. Her small fingers gripped the wood, her palms biting into the splinters.

The door groaned as it opened.

A shadow filled the doorway.

Tall. Motionless. Watching.

A sob built in her throat, but she swallowed it down, her body shaking so violently she thought she might break.

The figure stepped forward, the dim light catching on something in their hand.

A key.

Her breath came in short, sharp gasps as she shrank as far back as she could.

Chapter 3

The shadow figure stepped forward, the floorboards creaking softly beneath their weight. The dim bulb overhead flickered as the shadow figure struck the switch by the door, casting long, uneven shadows that stretched across the walls like twisted fingers, reaching for her.

The air in the room was thick, too still, too quiet, pressing against her skin like an invisible hand choking the breath from her.

She shivered, curling herself into an even tighter ball against the far side of the cage, her thin dress doing nothing to keep the chill away.
Her breath caught in her throat, her chest rising and falling too quickly, panic still gripping her.

The shadow man didn't speak.

He didn't move beyond that final step.

He just stood there, towering over the cage, uncaring, unmoving, unreadable.

200

She clenched her jaw, swallowing back another sob.
Tears burned in her eyes, her throat raw from screaming, her voice lost somewhere between desperation and exhaustion.

Her fingers twitched against the bars. If he had come to hurt her, wouldn't he have done it by now? If he had come to let her go, why wasn't he moving?

What did he want?

Her body trembled violently, her fingers curled into the comfort of her dress, gripping the material as though it might ground her.

The silence stretched between them, deep and endless.

Her gaze flickered up through damp lashes, barely able to make out his form in the dim light. The figure was tall, his shoulders broad beneath the long coat he wore. His face was still hidden in the shadows, shrouded in mystery, his very presence suffocating.

And yet...

He did nothing.

No words. No movement.

Just watched.

She exhaled shakily, her fingers slowly loosening their grip. There was nothing left in her. The fight, the screaming, the desperate shaking of the cage; it had drained her, hollowed her out like an empty shell.

She pressed her forehead against the wooden slats, her skin cool against the rough surface. Her limbs felt heavy, her body aching from the cold, her muscles tight from tension.

She felt her breathing slow.
Her eyelids droop.

She was losing the battle against exhaustion, her body giving in to the fatigue that wrapped around her like chains.

Her fingers twitched one last time—then stilled.

Her chest rose and fell, her breath growing quieter.

The shadow man didn't move.

He only watched as she finally succumbed to sleep.

Chapter 4

She dreamed of sky.

Not the suffocating darkness of the room, not the oppressive weight of the cage, but sky.

Wide and endless, a brilliant blue that stretched in every direction. Wisps of clouds drifted lazily across it, golden with sunlight, their edges soft and feathered.

Wind rushed past her, warm and gentle, tangling in her hair as she ran. The warmth of the sun on her skin warming her as she reached and stretched her face to the sky.

Bare feet on soft grass, cool and damp with morning dew. The earth beneath her felt alive, full of possibility. She didn't know where she was going, didn't care—because she was free.

Her heart raced, not with fear, but with exhilaration. Her arms stretched out; her breath came easy, deep and full.

She wasn't trapped.

The cage didn't exist here. The dark, musty room, the creaking door, the shadow figure standing beside her—none of it was real.

Only the sky.

Only the wind.

Only the sun.

Only freedom.

She laughed, a bright, weightless sound.

She belonged here, beneath the open sky, flying beneath the golden sun.

And then—

Something changed.

A shift in the wind. A stillness that hadn't been there before as she looked ahead, she saw it far

in the distance at first then closer until there
was no mistaking it.
A shadow, that stretched across the grass.

Tall. Cold. Familiar.

The laughter faded from her lips.

She crashed down. The world around her grew
dim, the blue sky darkening at the edges. The
golden light cooled, losing its warmth.

The shadow reached for her.

Watching.
Waiting.

A whisper of breath against her ear. Her
stomach twisted, her skin prickling with unease.
The grass beneath her feet wasn't soft anymore.
It felt... brittle. Sharp. Painful.

She turned her head slowly, her breath catching
in her throat.

The shadow loomed, its form stretching unnaturally across the ground, swallowing the green, bleeding into the sky absorbing the entire world.
How was he here? This is her one chance to escape, her one chance to feel.

Even in sleep, he had followed her.

Even in her dreams, she wasn't free.

A cold dread wrapped around her, tight and suffocating.

She tried to run—but her feet wouldn't move.

The sky grew darker. The wind vanished.

And then

The dream shattered.

She woke with a gasp; the wooden bars still pressed against her skin. The room was still dark, the air still heavy and foul.

And the shadow figure, he was still there.

Watching.
Waiting.

Chapter 5

She continued her micro sleeps for what felt like days, wondering when the shadow man would do something. Until the day she woke to pain. A deep, aching soreness that settled into her bones, into every muscle, into the very core of her being. Her head throbbed, her limbs were stiff, and her stomach twisted with a hollow, gnawing hunger.

For a moment, she didn't move.

Didn't open her eyes.

She lay curled in the wooden cage, the cold wooden slats pressing into her skin through the thin fabric of her dress. The damp scent of the room filled her nostrils—old wood, stale air, something metallic and sour.

She felt... weak and pathetic.

Wrong.

Her mouth was dry, her lips cracked. Her skin felt clammy, sticky with sweat and dirt, her dark hair was tangled and stiff with filth. She could feel it clinging to her scalp, the strands knotted and matted.

A sickness coiled in her gut.

She swallowed, the motion painful, her throat raw from crying, from screaming. But no sound came now.

Just silence.

And then—movement.

A shift in the air. A presence. His presence.

Her eyelids fluttered open, sluggish, her vision blurring before sharpening onto him. The shadow man.

He stood just beyond the bars, watching, always watching. His face was still obscured beneath the hood of his long coat, his posture eerily still.

A wave of fear crawled up her spine, but her body was too heavy, too exhausted to react the way it should. Her breath quickened, but her limbs refused to obey.

The shadow man moved.

Without warning, he reached for the cage.

The sound of wood groaning, the creak of rope unravelling. A snap—then suddenly, the slats holding her in place gave way, falling open.

She barely had time to process before hands were on her.

Large, strong hands, fingers digging into her thin arms, lifting her as if she weighed nothing.

She let out a sharp gasp, but no sound came.

Her mind screamed at her to fight, to bite, punch, kick, but her body was useless, helpless in his grip.

She tried to twist away, but his hold was unyielding. The motion sent a wave of dizziness crashing through her, the world tilting violently.

Her stomach churned.

The shadow man didn't pause.

He carried her easily, his grip firm. His coat smelled of damp and something earthy, something unfamiliar. She was nothing in his arms. A rag doll. A plaything.

He said something—low, guttural, foreign.

The words slid through the air like thick oil, meaningless to her ears, yet weighted.

She flinched, her breathing coming in quick, shallow gasps.

He didn't stop. Through the doorway, out of the room, down a narrow, dimly lit hall. The walls were faded, the wallpaper peeling in long, curling strips. The wooden floor groaned beneath his steps, dust rising in the stagnant air.

The house smelled of rot. A home long ago forgotten.

She barely had time to take it in before they reached another door. A heavy one.

He pushed it open with ease.

The bathroom.

She saw it all at once—the grimy clawfoot tub, the rusted sink, the cracked tiles covered in filth. The air was damp, heavy with moisture, a faint scent of mildew clinging to every surface.

The bathtub was already full.

Water.

Dark, murky and waiting.

She stiffened in his grip, her fingers twitching weakly against his coat. She tried to shake her head, but the motion was barely there, a useless flicker.

No. No, No, No.

She whimpered as he moved toward the tub.

More words. That same, unfamiliar language.

Then, he stripped her. The air hit her skin, cold and sharp like the edge of a knife. Her breath stolen, her hands weakly grasping at nothing, trying to cover, to hide, to escape.

She was too slow. Too weak.

He lifted her, his grip never faltering—then dropped her.

She hit the water with a sharp splash, her body seizing at the sudden shock.

Cold.

So cold.

It rushed over her, into her nose, her mouth, filling every inch of her, drowning her in filth.

She gasped, choking on the taste of it—metallic, dirty.

The bath reeked.

Not just of mildew, but something else.

Something faintly sour.

Something that made her heave, her empty stomach trying to bring something up, even bile would be better than the painful wretches her stomach made in a pitiful attempt at emptying.

Her poor body fought against her tightening muscles, retracting; her arms flailed weakly. She tried to resist, to escape, to fight, but his hands were already on her again.

Holding her down.

And then—

Scrubbing.

Rough. Violent. A hard rock-shaped object dragged across her skin, scraping away layers of grime, sweat, and skin. She let out a muffled cry, the pressure unbearable. Her skin burned, rubbed raw beneath the relentless motion. Pain like she had never known, biting at her skin like it was on fire.

His hands continued moving without hesitation—scrubbing, forcing, stripping her down to nothing. It felt like he had scrubbed all her skin away, blood seeping out of every pore. The object began moving over her arms, shoulders, and neck.

She turned her head away, a whimper escaping her lips.

He didn't stop.

More words. That same low, guttural voice.

She squeezed her eyes shut, her body curling inward, trying to escape the torment and pain. She didn't want to hear him. She didn't want to know what he was saying. She just wanted it to end. Tears stung her eyes, but she refused to show him weakness.

The object scraped over her ribs, down her legs, over every inch of her until her skin felt open, raw and exposed, small welts left all over her body. He had scrubbed her until there was nothing left. Until she was clean and new.

Then, just as suddenly as it started, it was over. The pressure lifted. The hands retreated.

She barely had a moment to catch her breath before she was lifted again. The frigid air hitting her like a Mack truck.

A rough towel wrapped around her—thin, threadbare, useless against the chill.

She trembled, her teeth chattering, her breath hitching in quiet, broken sobs.

She could still feel the phantom scrubbing on her skin, the raw sting of it lingering long after his hands were gone. Her body belonged to her again— but it didn't feel like hers anymore.

She was carried out of the bathroom, her damp skin sticking to the fabric of the towel as he moved her down another hallway, through another door.

A mattress, thin sheets. The room was just as bare, empty, except for the mattress on the floor.

She was placed down, the towel removed, and replaced with something new.

A gown, too big and too thin to be of any use.

A whisper of fabric against her still-damp skin.

He pulled the covers over her, but they did nothing to stop the cold.

She curled into herself, her breath uneven, her mind swimming in the overwhelming sensations of it all.

The shadow man stood over her for a long moment.

Watching.

Always watching.

More words—softer this time.

Almost gentle.

Then, he turned and left, clicking the lock
behind him.

Darkness swallowed the room. She lay there,
staring at nothing, her body too drained, too
battered to move. Her skin still burned, her
muscles ached, her mind reeled.

And deep in the pit of her stomach, she dreaded
tomorrow.

Chapter 6

She was woken by hands.
They were on her before she could register
anything.

Rough fingers clamped around her wrist,
yanking her upward. The thin blanket tangled
around her legs, dragging along the floor as she
was hauled to her feet. Her body felt too heavy,
her limbs like lead, her muscles aching from the
endless cycle of fear and exhaustion.

The shadow man was there. Always there.

Towering. Silent. Watching.

His grip was firm and impersonal. His fingers
pressed against the thin skin of her body like she
were an object, a thing to be carried.

Her lips parted, but no sound came. What was
the point? There was no room left for
screaming. No fight left in her.

The thin gown clung to her, offering no warmth,
no protection. Her hair, still damp from the

scrubbing, stuck to her skin, sending shivers down her spine.

She tried to twist away. Just a little.

Just enough to feel like she had chosen something—even if it was only this.

His grip tightened.

A warning.

She didn't try again.

They moved through the house, the air thick and stale. The walls crumbled, and the wallpaper peeled in long, curling strips.

The whole house felt sick.

And then, ahead of her voice.

Too many voices.

Low murmurs. Laughter. The sound of cups being set on wooden surfaces.

They were close. Her stomach clenched painfully, nausea clawing its way up her throat.

A door creaked open. Then she saw them. All of them. And every single one of them turned to stare at her.

It was too full.

The air was thick with the sound of them, of their breathing, their shifting bodies, their voices.

The shadow man placed her on a long wooden table, with plates and cups scattered the remnants of a meal still littering the surface. The fireplace in the corner was cold, the bricks blackened with soot. The chairs were mismatched; some were old and cracked, and others were newer.

And then—

The eyes.

Dozens of them.

Watching her. Some were narrowed, inspecting. Some were wide with curiosity. Some... hungry.

She couldn't breathe.

Her body locked, frozen beneath their stares, her limbs stiff, her chest too tight to allow air.

She didn't belong here.

She belonged anywhere but here.

A low murmur rippled through the crowd—a language she didn't understand.

Words tangled, rough, rolling off their tongues with practised ease, too sharp, too foreign.

She flinched as the first hand reached for her.

Cold fingers brushed against her cheek.

She jerked back, but another set of hands followed.

Fingertips pressing against her jaw, tilting her head.

Measuring.

Testing.

A thumb dragged across her bottom lip, a slow, deliberate motion.

A sharp gasp escaped her throat, her body twisting instinctively—but she couldn't escape them.

More hands followed.

Grabbing. Prodding.

Pressing at her arms, her shoulders, her ribs.

A man pinched the skin on her forearm, testing the thinness of it.

A woman ran her hands over her collarbones, her nails scraping against her too-prominent bones.

And then—

A boy.

No older than seven.

He stepped forward, his small hand fisting into her hair—and pulled.

Hard.

She let out a muffled whimper, her head snapping back, her scalp burning.

Laughter.

Sharp and cruel.

She trembled, her body locked in place, her breath ragged and broken.

They weren't just touching her.

They were evaluating her.

She was livestock at a market.

Like she wasn't human at all.

Her fingers curled into weak fists, helpless, nails pressing into her own skin as if she could somehow disappear inside herself.

She wanted to vanish.

To sink through the floor, to become nothing at all.

Their voices were louder now, overlapping, clashing, their words incomprehensible.

Her heartbeat pounded in her ears, drowning them out, drowning out everything.

And then—

A sharp clap.

Everything stopped.

The hands withdrew.

The voices fell into a hush.

The shift in the air was immediate, thick with expectation.

She sucked in a shaky breath, her chest rising and falling too fast, too unevenly.

A chair scraped against the floor.

Someone stood.

She didn't dare look at first, her gaze fixed on the worn wooden planks beneath her feet.

Then—boots.

Dark, polished.

Not the shadow man.

Someone else.

She forced herself to lift her head, her movements slow, sluggish.

A man.

Older. Larger. Different.

His coat was heavier than the others, the fabric thick, well-made. His hair was grey at the temples, his features sharp, his eyes dark and unreadable.

But he wasn't looking at her.

He was looking at the shadow man.

A conversation began.

Low, deliberate words passed between them, their voices steady, measured.

The older man's gaze flickered to her every so often, assessing, calculating.

The shadow man responded with short, clipped answers.

It was a discussion.

A transaction.

Her stomach twisted violently.

She didn't need to understand the words.

She already knew what they meant.

228

Her hands trembled at her side, her throat tight
with the weight of helplessness.

They were deciding what to do with her.

Where she would go.

Who she would belong to.

She was nothing but a thing.

And no matter how badly she wanted to run,
fight, or scream. She had no say. Not anymore.

Then, a loud cheering sounded as everyone
turned to stare at her.
Was she sold? Was she staying? She would
never understand them.

Chapter 7

Time had lost all meaning.

No windows. No clocks. No change in the light.

Just emptiness.

The walls surrounded her, blank and cracked, trapping her with their silence. The wooden floor was hard beneath her, rough against her bare skin, the cold seeping into her bones.

She had given up trying to count the days.

Had given up trying to stay awake when exhaustion pulled at her.

Had given up screaming when her throat burned raw.

Her body was failing. She had just given up.

She felt it in the way her limbs refused to move sometimes, in the way her stomach twisted into painful knots, in the way her mind had begun to slip into something distant, detached.

The first few days—if they had even been days—she had fought.

She had banged against the door until her knuckles split, had thrown herself against the wood until her shoulders ached, had scratched at the peeling wallpaper until her fingers were raw.

She had called out, begged, screamed.

But the house had swallowed her voice whole.

And no one had come.

She had learned quickly that her energy was a precious thing.

She couldn't waste it.

Couldn't let herself burn out too quickly.

So, she had stopped moving.

Stopped crying.

Stopped thinking about anything except staying alive.

The only time the door opened was when they brought her milk.

Not food. Never food.

Just a single, dusty plastic bottle, filled with something warm, sour, thick on her tongue.

Always left on the floor, just beyond her reach.

Always at the last moment, when the edges of her vision blackened, when her body trembled so hard, she could barely lift her head.

She told herself she wouldn't drink it.

That she would rather starve than take what they gave her.

But in the end, she always did.

Her hands would shake as she reached for it, her fingers slipping against the bottle, her stomach cramping from hunger so badly that she thought she might break apart.

She hated the feeling of relief that came when the liquid slid down her throat. Hated the way her body clung to life, even when she yearned to let go.

And then the waiting would begin again.

For the next time the door creaked open.

For the next time she would be given just enough to keep her from the eternal peace she craved.

As she sat in the corner, her arms wrapped around her knees, her ribs protruding from her skin. Making her gown hang off her like the fabric draped over a halloween skeleton.

She felt hollow, empty.

The last time he had brought her milk, he had made a mistake. A small thing. A nothing thing.

But her eyes locked onto it, her mind snapping sharp, her fingers twitching with the first hint of hope she had felt in weeks.

He had forgotten to take the bottle.

It sat there, abandoned, after she had drained it.

Glass. Thick. Solid. Breakable.

A single thread of thought unravelled inside her mind.

Her fingers closed around it, her palm pressing against the cool, smooth surface.

A weapon.

It wasn't much.

She was starving, weak, broken.

But desperation was its own kind of strength.

If she could hide it, keep it tucked away where he wouldn't see—

She could wait. Wait for the door to open.

Wait for the moment when he was close enough, distracted enough, unguarded.

Then she could strike.

One perfect hit to the head. Or the neck.

Just enough to stun the shadow man.

Just enough to run.

Her breath came faster, her heart hammering for the first time in so long.

Something had returned to her.

Something she had almost forgotten.

Hope.

The will to live.

Her fingers tightened around the bottle. She had one chance.

One chance to escape.

One chance to survive.

And when the door opened again—

She would be ready.

Chapter 8

She didn't hear him coming, slipping in and out of sleep, curled against the hard wooden floor, her arms wrapped weakly around her body. The sharp edges of her ribs pressed into her skin, her gown hanging loose from her bony frame.

Her fingers twitched as she fought to stay awake, to stay aware.

The empty milk bottle was still hidden beneath her gown, the only thing she had—her only plan.

Then came the hands. Grabbing. Lifting.

Her eyes flew open, her heart slamming against her ribs as rough fingers hauled her up, dragging her out of the room before she could even struggle.

She gasped; her limbs were too weak to fight. The world spun, her vision blurred from hunger, exhaustion, and nothingness.

She expected another bath. Another round of scrubbing, stripping, touching.

But instead—

A new room.

The moment she was shoved inside, she stilled.

She wasn't alone.

A girl sat on the far side of the small room, her back against the wall, legs drawn up to her chest.
She was older. Her dark hair was a tangled, mottled mess around her sunken face, her skin pale, making her eyes seem like deep pits of nothingness.

She wasn't afraid. She was watching.

Not with cruelty. But with curiosity.

Just watching. Why was everyone always just watching?

The door slammed shut behind her.

238

The new girl exhaled, then said something—

The language.

That language was wrong, different, and scary.

Her body locked up.

She flinched back, pressing herself against the door, her breath coming in sharp, uneven gasps.

That language. The shadow man's language.

The new girl—Bella—noticed.

Her words faltered, and she stared at her for a long moment.

Then she said something else.

A single word.

Soft. Careful.

Her name.

Bella had said her name.

Days passed.

Or only hours.

Bella talked. She didn't.

Sometimes Bella sounded like she was telling a story. Other times, she murmured, as if speaking was a habit she couldn't break.

She wanted to hate her for it.

For speaking their language.

For sitting so calmly when they were both trapped.

But she couldn't. Bella wasn't cruel. Bella didn't touch her. Bella didn't demand anything.

She just existed. And that was more than she had been given in so long.

She watched Bella.

She watched how she moved.

How they treated her.

And she realised something.

Bella had more freedom.

The door didn't always lock when Bella was alone.

Bella could help her.

For the first time in weeks, she spoke.

A whisper.

A single word.

"Help."

Bella's gaze snapped to hers, surprised.

She hesitated.

Then—she shook her head.

No.

Her chest tightened.

She tried again, her voice urgent, her fingers curling into weak fists.

"Please."

Bella's expression darkened. Not with cruelty, with pity.

She shook her head again.

"No."

Panic clawed up her throat.

She grabbed Bella's wrist.

Bella stilled.

Their eyes met.

And for the first time, Bella looked scared too.

Then—

A sound.

A footstep.

Both girls went still.

The door opened.

The shadow man.

He stepped inside, towering, his presence suffocating.

Bella tensed beside her.

And then—

He spoke.

That same low, unreadable tone.

But this time, he wasn't speaking to her.

He was speaking to Bella.

Bella answered.

Her voice was steady, controlled—but there was something beneath it.

Something tight.

She didn't understand the words, but she understood the moment.

She had spoken to Bella. And now, Bella was being removed.

The shadow man reached for her. Bella didn't fight.

She simply stood.

Bella turned once—her dark eyes locking onto hers, something almost apologetic flashing behind them.

Then she was gone.

The door shut behind them.

And she was alone again.

It felt like Bella had never been there at all.

Had she had imagined it.

She stared at the empty space Bella had left behind, her chest rising and falling too fast, too hard.

They had taken her away.

Because she had spoken to her.

Because she had tried to escape.

And now Bella was gone.

She was alone again.

And for the first time since she had woken in this god forsaken place—

She felt fear not just for herself, but for someone else, perhaps even an ally or even a possible friend.

Chapter 9

The next time she woke the air was biting cold, every movement was like ice branding itself into her skin. Her cheek was pressed to it, her breath fogging a small patch beneath her lips. She tried to remember how she got here—but the memories were smeared, bleeding at the edges like ink dropped in water. Something had been done to her. Something inside her head.

She tried to lift her hand.

Nothing.

She tried again. A twitch. Her fingers trembled— barely a flutter, but it was a start.

Somewhere, she could smell the coppery smell of blood, her stomach turned. She shifted her eyes instead of her head. The light above buzzed faintly, a naked bulb swinging gently from a frayed cord. Shadows slipped along the walls in slow, hypnotic arcs.

And in the deepest of them stood him.

The Shadow Man.

He was almost part of the wall at first. A shape darker than the dark, tall and silent. His outline was loose, like someone had blurred him on purpose. He didn't move. Didn't blink. Just watched.

She hated how much he watched.

Every move she made—every failed attempt to lift her arm, every shallow breath—felt catalogued, filed away behind that unreadable gaze. He was patient. Too patient. Like he had all the time in the world to watch her unravel.

Then came the voice.

"Oh no, don't get up on my account."

It was smooth, sardonic, and female.

Bella.

The woman's footsteps were sharp, she strutted into view like she owned the place, arms folded across her chest. She was dressed in mismatched clothes—men's trousers cinched with a belt, a dirty white singlet that clung to her thin frame.

Bella crouched beside her with a cluck of her tongue.

"You look like a broken marionette," she said, tapping her cheek with two fingers. Not hard—but enough to make the woman's skin sting. Maybe the drugs were wearing off? Why was she so weak, it must be drugs sapping her strength.

Bella's lips parted, dry as paper. A rasp escaped, but no words.

Bella leaned closer, voice dropping to a whisper. "Let me guess. Your arms are like jelly. Your legs are screaming. Your head's full of fog." She smiled with teeth too white for her stained fingertips.

Ok, so that was good. That means I'm waking up, I'll be strong soon and able to finally escape.

With immense effort, she rolled onto her side. Her shoulder flared with pain. Her limbs were leaden, but her instincts screamed to move, crawl, run—anything. Her elbow dragged across the floor. The movement was pathetic, but it was hers.

She gritted her teeth. Inch by inch.

"Oooooh," Bella cooed, standing again. "The little lamb wants to leave the pen."

She didn't answer. Her eyes flicked toward the door. Was he there? She couldn't remember. All she saw were walls—peeling, cracked, stained with stains she didn't want to name.

The Shadow Man hadn't moved. Still rooted to the same spot. Still staring.

"What is he?" she rasped at last. Her voice was hoarse, barely more than a whisper.

Bella chuckled, as if that question amused her. "He's the one who decides if you're useful. Or if you're entertainment." She tilted her head. "Right now, you're kind of both."

The woman's knees finally bent. The pain was immense, stabbing through her thighs like knives, but she managed to prop herself onto all fours. Her arms shook under her own weight.

"Oh, look at you," Bella drawled. "Like a baby deer. You want to stand, don't you? Do you think you might make it to that hallway if you get enough strength in those legs? Maybe there's a door? Maybe there's a window?"

She didn't look at Bella. She focused on the floor. Her breath hitched with each push forward. Her body was drenched in cold sweat.

One crawl.
Then another.
Then another.

Her skin burned where it touched the ground, but pain meant sensation. Sensation meant her body was coming back.

"I'm not staying here," she hissed.

Bella grinned. "Oh, you'll leave eventually. Either walking or dragged."

The Shadow Man finally moved. Not a step—but a tilt. His head leaned just slightly, like a predator considering the moment to strike. Or perhaps... curious.

She stopped crawling. Not in defeat—but in calculation. Her right hand curled into a fist. Her fingers were working now. Weak, but working.

Not yet. But soon.

The rage was growing. It bloomed in her chest like a second heartbeat, wild and hot.

They thought she would break.

Let them watch.

When she stood, she would burn the memory of this crawl into their minds. When she ran, they would hear her footsteps in their sleep.

And when she returned—because she would return—she'd make them crawl.

Chapter 10

She marked time by the bulb's slow swing.

Back and forth.
Back and forth.
A dull rhythm above her, like a heartbeat
suspended in the ceiling.

There was no clock to chart her progress. Only
her body. Her breath. The ache in her bones.
The pull in her muscles. This was her
timekeeper now.

When she first crawled, it was survival. Dragging
herself to the far wall to escape the eyes, or
Bella's words, or the throb in her skull. But now,
after practicing for days, or perhaps only hours,
crawling had become the norm.

Every movement was deliberate.
Left hand forward.
Right knee.
Drag.
Pause.
Repeat.

The floor was a skin-shredder—cold, gritty, with puddles of some foul-smelling liquid. It had taken the top layers of her palms and carved red trails across her knees. Her skin wept with each shuffle, but the sting was a good sign. It meant she still felt. Still healed.

She'd stopped crying. She didn't scream. Her body was sore, her throat raw, but her mind was sharpening like glass. Somewhere inside, a quiet, cold determination had formed—calm as the sky before a storm.

Bella had noticed her progress.

She no longer hovered as much. On the first day, she had smirked and leaned against the far wall, arms folded, offering commentary with every breath.

"Oh how tragic, our little deer's legs won't work."

"Crawling's such a bad look, darling—have some dignity."

"Do you think this is a prison escape movie? Because spoiler alert: no one's coming."

But now, Bella only offered a passing glance and a furrow of her brow. Her smirk came slower. Her words quieter.

On the second day, she made it from the back wall to the edge of the room and back without collapsing. It had taken a long time. Her breathing came in short, sharp gasps, and sweat clung to her spine like icewater. But she had made it. Under her own power.

Bella was silent the whole time. Not mocking. Not amused. Just... silent. That silence was worth more than a thousand words. It was recognition. Fear, maybe. Or something worse.

Because Bella had stopped thinking she was broken.

After what seemed like forever, she began to pull herself up.

The wall was rough and pitted stone with the texture of dried blood and cracked cement. Her fingers gripped it, testing. She used her elbows, then her knees, anchoring her forehead against the wall as she rose an inch at a time. Her legs quivered violently. Her feet skidded, slipped, nearly gave out—but she didn't let them.

Her first time standing lasted three seconds.

The second: five.

By the fourth attempt, she stood for twenty-two seconds before she dropped, panting, onto her knees.

Each time she rose, something grew in her chest—like a lit coal. Not anger. Not pride. Something deeper. Something older. Survival.

The Shadow Man watched without blinking.

He hadn't moved since she started. Always there in the farthest shadow, too still to be natural. Sometimes she could almost forget he was real—until she moved too quickly, and he'd tilt his head like a spider feeling the vibration of prey.

But she no longer feared his gaze. She fed off it.

She was no longer just surviving.
She was training.

By the end of the fourth week—if it was indeed a fourth—she could walk. Not gracefully, and not far. Her steps were slow and awkward, and she wobbled like the ground beneath her shifted. But she crossed the room upright. Touched one wall. Turned. Crossed again.

One round. Then two.

Bella's voice had vanished completely. She sat in the corner now, chewing on stale bread, watching with something close to discomfort on her face.

"What are you doing?" she finally asked, her voice dull. "You're wasting your energy."

She didn't answer.

She kept walking. Turn. Walk. Turn. Walk.

Even when she stumbled, she didn't crawl back.
She caught the wall, steadied herself, and
continued.

She knew something Bella didn't:
The body remembers.
The body learns.

And soon, this room would no longer be enough
to hold her.

Later that night, under the silent hum of the
swaying bulb, the woman stood in the centre of
the room, hands by her sides, spine straight.

No crawling. No wall.

She didn't even shake.

The Shadow Man tilted his head again.

Bella didn't speak.

And for the first time, she smiled. A quiet, cracked smile. Small, but real.

Let them watch.

Let them whisper and wonder.

She was standing now.
And she was just getting started.

Chapter 11

The room had shrunk. Not in size, but in air. The tension made it feel smaller, tighter, like the walls leaned in a little more each time the two women crossed paths.

They didn't speak much anymore—not in full words. Not unless they had to.

But there was no mistaking it now: a rivalry had set in.

It wasn't loud. It wasn't fists or shouting. It was colder than that. Sharper. Like a wire strung between them, pulled taut, humming with every step, every breath. A war fought in glances and silences.

Bella had once owned this place, in her way, not with keys or chains, but with her mouth, swagger, and smirking cruelty. She walked like someone who knew she was untouchable. She'd been here longer—weeks, months, maybe even years. She knew how the Shadow Man worked. What amused him. What didn't.

She had become part of the room, like the cracked walls or the swinging bulb.

It had been all Bella until she had arrived.

She who crawled. She who cried. The one Bella expected to break within days. But she hadn't. She had risen.

Day by day, she had pulled herself from the floor. From her ruin. From the poison in her veins. She had rebuilt herself from the fingertips up—crawling, standing, walking, not with grace, but with purpose.

Bella watched it all, growing quieter with each of her steps.

Her jabs became fewer. The sarcasm dulled. The amusement faded.

And then came the look.

That first real look.

It happened when she crossed the room unaided, her shoulders square, her legs steady. Bella sat on the edge of her mattress, one knee tucked to her chest, her mouth slightly open.

Their eyes met.

Bella looked away first.

From then on, the game shifted.

Bella began mimicking strength. She stood more often and exercised in place. She pushed her own limits—but hers were born of pride, not survival. She wasn't rebuilding; she was defending.

She dropped barbed comments again, sharper now, with edges that cut closer to the bone.

"Don't think you're special just because you can stand. I can run. Doesn't help me."

"Keep pacing like that, and the shadow man will think you're trying to escape. You want to see what happens when he's not silent?"

She said nothing in return. She'd stopped feeding Bella's hunger for a reaction.
One morning, She rose early, standing silently at the far end of the room. She stretched slowly, testing her limbs, her breath fogging in the cold air.

Bella watched her from the shadows, chewing a strip of stale bread. Her jaw worked tightly.

"You think you're better than me now?" Bella asked suddenly.

The words hung in the air like frost.

She turned, face unreadable.

"No," she said softly. "I know I'm not like you."

Bella's eyes narrowed. "Careful. You don't know what this place does yet. You're still new. Still pretending it's a game you can win."

She stepped forward slowly, her back straight.

"I'm not playing a game," she said. "You are. You've been playing for so long you've forgotten how to fight."

It was the closest thing to a threat she'd ever spoken aloud.

The Shadow Man shifted in the corner, his body a silent blur. He was always there watching. Judging.

Bella's jaw tensed. She stood quickly and moved to the other side of the room, but her steps were uneven now. Her silence was thick with something sour.

The balance had tipped.

They were wolves now—caged, circling. One had ruled through cruelty, the other through grit.

And they both knew:

264

This room wasn't big enough for both of them to survive.

Chapter 12

The next time the shadow man came for her, she gave in, followed his lead. She was going to try to be a good obedient captive, she might get some more freedom like Bella. Hopefully, the punishment would be less severe.

This time, he grabbed her neck, fastening a rope around her shoulders with surprising speed, speaking in a guttural tone, he grunted at her to move.

She just stood there blankly,

The shadow man clearly wasn't in any mood to wait and dragged her behind him, descending the porch steps deep into the woods.

She didn't know how long they had walked. The trees stretched endlessly, the trail winding through the damp wood, swallowing them whole. She stopped trying to guess time, stopped trying to count her steps—the only things that mattered were the rope around her, the dull ache in her bare feet, and the slow, steady pull of the shadow man forcing her forward.

Her breath came shallow and quiet, misting in the freezing air.

The shadow man walked beside her, his presence a weight she could not escape.

And then, without warning—

The woods opened into a clearing hidden deep among the trees, where no one would ever find it. Tree stumps sat low and uneven, some sagging with age and damp.

A fire burned at the centre, its smoke curling thick and grey into the air. Around it, people.

Men. Women. Children.

Talking, eating, working. Existing.

Like this was normal. Like this was home.

She stumbled slightly, her legs nearly giving out at the sight.

And yet all she felt was fear; this wasn't a rescue. This was something worse.

The shadow man released her rope letting it out, He shouted a short, sharp word, and suddenly—all eyes turned toward her.

It happened so fast.

The moment they saw her, the moment they saw the bindings, the leash, the way she was led like an animal—

The air changed.

People moved toward her, stepping out of their places around the fire, from the porches of the buildings, from the shadows.

Her chest tightened.

She wanted to run.

But the leash held her still.

They surrounded her.

A ring of faces, all staring, studying.

Murmuring.

Speaking that language—the one she could never understand, thick with rough sounds, heavy syllables, guttural inflections.

She swallowed hard.

Her breath shook.

She tried to make herself small, her shoulders curling inward, her wrists pulling weakly against the rope.

It didn't matter.

They still touched her, fingers pressed against her arms, feeling the thinness of her skin, the bones beneath.

Someone ran a hand down her spine, a slow, measuring touch that sent a shudder through her entire body.

A woman lifted her chin, examining her teeth, turning her head side to side like she was nothing more than an object to be appraised.

She let out a sharp breath, trying to pull back, but more hands followed—

Grasping her wrists.

Pressing against her ribs.

Testing the weight of her.

A man murmured something, then reached out, touched her stomach, her hip, inching lower.

She jerked away, a sharp, instinctual movement—the first real movement she had made in days. And the response was immediate.

A hand in her hair, fingers twisting and yanking, pulling her head back sharply.

She let out a small cry, her throat too dry, too hoarse to make it louder. Laughter rippled through the group.

Not cruel laughter.

Not mocking.

But something casual. Indifferent.

Like she was just the latest thing to be played with.

To them she wasn't a person at all, so what was the point.

She stopped fighting.

Stopped moving.

Her body went still, her breath coming in shallow, uneven gasps.

She let them do it, hopefully it would be over soon.

Let them pull at her hair, touch her skin, prod her arms, measure the length of her fingers.

Because resisting did nothing.

Because fighting did nothing.

Because the moment she flinched, the moment she showed fear, they laughed again—like she was their entertainment.

Her vision blurred with the sheer weight of it.

The hands. The voices.

She felt sick.

Then—a voice.

Not one from the crowd.

Not one of the men who had taken her from the woods.

The older man.

The one from before, the one who had stood at the table and spoken to the shadow man.

His voice cut through the murmuring, through the laughter, through the words she couldn't understand.

The hands stopped.

The people stilled.

He spoke again, his words measured, final. The people cheered.

Her stomach twisted painfully.

She didn't need to understand their words.

She already knew.

They were deciding what would happen to her next.
She twisted just slightly, her hands pulling weakly at the rope, her feet shifting on the damp earth.

The movement was small.

So small.

But the shadow man noticed.

His eyes snapped to hers, sharp. Watching.

He took a single step forward.

Her body locked up.

The air stilled.

She knew what he was telling her, even without words.

You will not run.

You will not fight.

You are nothing.

You are mine.

And as the weight of those silent words settled in her bones, her chest caved inward—

She realised, for the first time, she believed them.

Chapter 13

The woods groaned low around them. Trees leaned inward, closing behind her, sealing off the path behind her like a wound scabbing over.

Her skin still crawled from their touch. The way they had circled her in that clearing, heads tilting just slightly, arms hanging loose. No one spoke. Not even the Shadow Man. He had only stood in the mist, a void in human shape, and *watched.*

One of them—maybe the tall woman with limp hair—had cupped her chin and stared into her eyes for a long time. She hadn't said yes. She hadn't said no. She had just let go and nodded toward the cabin.

She tried not to cry, but her throat ached from holding it in. Her hands were shaking. She didn't ask questions because no one would answer them.

The door creaked open, yawning like a mouth too old to chew. Inside, the cabin was dark, colder than she remembered, but she knew better than to hesitate. She stepped over the threshold barefoot and hollow.

The door closed behind her.

She stood there, alone.

No one came.

No voice barked orders.

No chores were listed.

The Shadow Man watched.

The silence was unbearable.

Was she a failure? Was she broken stock? Was she going to be given to someone—or something—else? For what? Labor? Ritual? Play? Did they sell girls like her by weight or by silence? Did the Shadow Man have brothers?

The thought of being passed from hand to hand like an object, like a toy, weakened her knees. She sat hard on the floor, back against the wall, arms around her middle like she could keep herself from falling apart.

The room felt smaller.

The air, heavier.

A sob escaped her lips.

She had tried so hard to stay invisible. To obey. To clean without being seen. To pass their inspection. And now, she was back here. No purpose given. No punishment declared.

The waiting was the worst.

Something was coming for her.

Not to take her. Not to punish. Not even to own.

To *decide*.

She buried her face in her knees, shaking. In the dark, she whispered:

"Please... please just tell me what I am."

But the house said nothing.

Because it wasn't meant to *tell*.

Only to keep.

Chapter 14

The room breathed around her. She felt it in the walls—the slow, quiet exhale of something waiting. Watching.

It was a stillness unlike any before. The kind of stillness that didn't just fill the air—it pressed on it. A silence so complete it hummed behind her ears. Her fingers were curled tight in her lap, nails bitten raw, body hunched forward on the mattress as if she might fold in on herself entirely.

Then she saw it.

The door.

It was always shut. Always locked from the outside with the unmistakable clang of bolts and iron. But now... it wasn't.

It sat slightly ajar, cracked open by a mere inch. No clang. No lock.

Her breath caught in her throat.

For a long moment she didn't move, didn't blink, as if her staring alone might slam it shut again. Her mind raced in spirals.

Was it a test? A mistake? A trick?

She slowly pushed herself off the mattress, her legs trembling. The ache from the last trial still lived in her bones, a dull throb in her shoulder and ribs. But pain was irrelevant now. Escape glimmered before her like water in the desert.

Her bare feet touched the cold floor. She winced but didn't stop. She crept toward the door, each step measured, each movement silent. The floorboards moaned faintly beneath her weight, but she kept moving, slow as breath.

Her fingers brushed the edge of the door. The cold metal bit into her skin, grounding her in the moment. She held her breath, pushed the door just a little farther open—two inches now. Then three.

No sound. No alarm. No footsteps.

She slipped through like smoke.

The hallway beyond was colder than her room. Narrow and lined with splintered wood panels, the corridor stretched in both directions, every corner swathed in shadow. There were no windows—just one flickering light overhead and the scent of mold, dust, and something faintly metallic.

She moved low, keeping her body close to the walls, ears straining for the slightest noise. Every creak of wood beneath her felt deafening. Every breath might give her away. Her heart thudded so loudly she feared it would alert someone.

At one point, she froze mid-step, hearing the soft rattle of chains from somewhere distant— maybe below her? Maybe behind a wall? She didn't wait to find out. She ducked into a shadowed alcove and pressed herself flat, swallowing down panic.

Minutes passed. Or maybe seconds. She wasn't sure.

Eventually, she crept on.

The cabin was bigger than she'd thought. Hallways branched off like a maze, doors led to empty rooms with cracked tiles and decaying furniture. Dust motes floated like ghosts in the flickering light.

Then—there. At the end of a long hall. A door.

Different. It looked... real. Not a room. Not a test. A way out. Wooden, weathered, with a bolt lock hanging open.

Beyond it, she could see the outline of trees, the faint shimmer of moonlight on dew.

Freedom.

Her pulse surged. Hands shaking, she approached. Her fingers reached for the handle. Turned it.

The door creaked open.

A breath of forest air hit her face—earthy, wet, alive.

Her foot crossed the threshold.

And then—stillness.

A shadow detached itself from the darkness to her right.

He had been there the whole time.

The Shadow Man.

He moved with impossible silence, too tall for the hallway, his limbs just a shade too long, too fluid. Her mouth opened in a silent scream. She stumbled backward, turned to run—

But he was already there.

She barely had time to gasp before his hands closed around her waist—cold and iron-strong. He lifted her effortlessly, her legs kicking, arms flailing.

"No—no, please—please!" she screamed. "I wasn't running—I wasn't—I just wanted to see—please!"

He didn't speak. He never did.

His grip was final. Steady. Like she weighed nothing.

He carried her back through the hallway, past the doors and shadows and splinters. The air grew colder with every step.

He didn't take her to the mattress.

He took her to the cage.

It stood in the centre of her room—welded metal bars, just tall enough to sit, too low to stand. The door yawned open like a waiting mouth.

"No… please not that—don't—don't put me in there!"

Her voice cracked. Her hands pushed against him, but it was like fighting stone.

He placed her inside, crouched down to meet her gaze for a moment—no face, no eyes, but she felt him watching.

Then the door clanged shut.

The lock clicked once. Quiet. Final.

He left.

The door closed behind him without sound.

And then—silence again.

Not the expectant kind.

The cruel kind.

She sat in the centre of the cage, too stunned to move. Her body trembled violently, and her forehead dropped to the bars.

Everything in her began to unravel.

Tears slid down her cheeks without sobs. Her breath came in short, shallow gasps. Her nails dug into her own arms, as if trying to feel something—anything—that wasn't this.

She whispered to the empty room.

"I was so close…"

She curled onto her side like a child. The cage was cold beneath her. Hard.

The door. The trees. The freedom. It had all been real. For a moment, she had touched it.

And now… it was gone.

The walls around her felt tighter. The shadows deeper.

And for the first time, truly, she wondered if escape had ever been possible at all…

Or if this was exactly what they wanted—

Hope.
Then despair.
Then nothing.

She lay still. The bars pressed against her back.
The silence roared.

And the fight inside her flickered.

Chapter 15

They returned her quietly, like she wasn't worth the noise.

The door creaked open in the dim half-light, and she was ushered inside with a firm, silent hand. No force, no shove. Just placed back where she belonged. Like a forgotten possession. Like a tool that had failed a test and was now shelved again until needed.

She didn't resist.

She couldn't.

Her legs moved because they had to, not because she willed them. Her head pounded with every heartbeat, a slow, dragging rhythm that drowned out her thoughts. Her mouth was dry. Her chest was tight. The sharp taste of vomit still clung to the back of her throat.

Her eyes adjusted slowly to the gloom.

Bella was awake.

She always was.

Sitting cross-legged on her mattress, arms wrapped around her knees, eyes shadowed but alert. The tin cup in her hands steamed faintly in the stale air. The scent of weak, lukewarm tea barely masked the metallic tang of blood and mold that haunted the room.

She looked up—slowly. Her eyes tracked the woman like a bird watching another fall from the sky.

"You got the cage."

It wasn't a question. Just fact. Heavy. Final.

The woman didn't answer. She swayed where she stood, then went to the edge of her mattress like her bones were made of glass. She sat with a slow, painful exhale and placed her hands in her lap to hide the shaking.

Bella didn't question her, just stared vacantly into the room.

288

Silence filled the space between them, thick and suffocating. Not peaceful. Not safe. Just full. Full of all the words neither of them wanted to say out loud.

Finally, she spoke, her voice so soft Bella almost missed it.

"I was so close."

Bella's gaze didn't change.

"I saw the trees," the woman went on. "I saw moonlight. I could smell the outside."

Her voice trembled. Saying it aloud made it worse. Like the memory might collapse if spoken too clearly.

"I touched the door handle," she whispered. "I opened it. I stepped through."

Bella's expression remained unreadable, but her grip on the cup tightened.

"And he was there."

The words came out like a confession.

"The Shadow Man."

Bella looked down at her drink. "He always is."

"I thought I had a chance," she said. "I wanted to believe they'd forgotten. That the door— maybe it was left open by mistake. Maybe..." She trailed off. "Maybe it wasn't even real."

She reached up and rubbed her forehead. The tears didn't come yet. Not fully. She felt them somewhere behind her eyes, but her body had learned not to waste water.

"They picked me up like I was nothing," she murmured. "Didn't even speak. Just carried me. And then... the cage."

Bella finally stood. She crossed the room in two slow steps and reached for the threadbare towel near the basin. She wet it, wrung it out, and tossed it toward her.

290

"Clean up," she muttered. "You're shaking like a kicked dog."

She caught it with clumsy hands and pressed it to her face, the cold water stinging her skin, waking her up just enough to remember she still existed. She wiped at the dried filth on her shirt, her cheek, her mouth. The movement felt pathetic—but necessary.

When she was done, she looked up at Bella, her eyes wide and haunted.

"Why are you still here?" she asked.

Bella blinked, slow and long. "What?"

"You've been here longer than me. You know more. You're stronger. Why haven't you tried?"

Bella let out a short, bitter laugh. "You think I haven't?"

She stared.

Bella moved to the corner, leaned against the wall, arms crossed tightly across her chest. She didn't meet the woman's eyes when she spoke next.

"You think I didn't run? That I didn't scream? That I didn't try the windows, the tunnels, the crawlspaces? You think I didn't try climbing the chimney like a bloody rat once?"

She laughed again.

"I tried everything."

She turned then, her expression darker, tired. "You know what I got for my effort? Punishment. Hunger. Silence. And the Shadow Man."

She looked away. "Eventually... you learn. You stop trying to escape. You start surviving instead."

The woman shook her head, the ache in her neck flaring.

292

"That's not survival," she said. "That's surrender."

Bella's eyes snapped to hers—sharp, defensive, wounded.

"You don't know what survival is yet," she hissed. "You think it's some noble act? That holding on to hope makes you brave?"

"It makes me human," the woman whispered.

They stared at each other. The air between them crackled.

Bella's mouth tightened. Her jaw worked like she wanted to say something else, something cruel or final, but couldn't find the words.

Then she slumped.

"You keep that hope too long," she said quietly, "and it turns on you. Starts whispering that things will change. That help is coming. That there's a door no one's watching." She looked at her over slowly. "And then you're back in the cage. Or worse."

"I have to believe," she said. "If I don't—what's left of me?"

Bella didn't answer. She sat back on her mattress and stared at the wall.

For the first time, she saw it—not anger. Not contempt.

Grief.

Bella had lost.

Bella had given up, just to keep breathing.

The silence stretched again.

But something had changed. Not trust—not yet. But something less cold. Something cracked.

They were no longer strangers in the same nightmare.

They were survivors in the different stages of giving up.

And now, maybe... they weren't entirely alone.

She lay back on her mattress, exhausted. Her muscles screamed. Her mind spun.

But somewhere deep inside, beneath the bruises, the pain, the defeat, a flicker still burned.

Small. Fragile.

But alive.

Hope.

And she wasn't ready to let it go.

Chapter 16

The door opened without warning.

The sound of it — that slow, heavy creak — snapped me awake like a slap. She was already sitting up before she meant to, heart hammering, eyes darting to the doorway.

He stood there.

The Shadow Man.

That towering silhouette, always still, always watching. Just his presence was enough to twist something cold into her stomach. The air in the room changed when he entered, like it knew what was coming before she did.

He didn't speak. He never needed to. A tilt of the head, a breath too long in silence — it was command enough.

Beside me, Bella stirred. She rubbed at her eyes and pushed herself up slowly. She didn't ask where we were going. Neither of us did. There was no point in asking questions. We weren't given answers.

The rope came next. He tied it around her shoulders like he always did — tight, unforgiving. The coarse fibres bit into her skin, reopening the red marks that had never healed.

Bella wasn't tied. She didn't need to be. She followed without resistance, Bella just followed on behind.

Every step forward felt like she was being pulled further from something real.

She couldn't stop shaking. Her teeth clenched so hard her jaw began to ache.

She didn't know where she was going. That was the worst part — *not knowing*. Not what was she going to be made to do? Just being led, blindly, deeper into the woods like an animal being walked to slaughter.

Then she reached the clearing. And forgot how to breathe.

The trees opened all at once, revealing a wide, perfect circle of space. At the centre was a dark and motionless pool, like a bottomless eye in the earth. It looked wrong, as if it wasn't water, just a giant cavern to the abyss.

And around it... people.

Dozens of them.

Standing. Sitting. Waiting. Laughing.

Until they saw her.

Then silence.

It dropped over the clearing like a lid.

All those faces turned. All those eyes locked on *her*.

She wanted to run, scream, turn and tear through the woods — but her legs wouldn't work. It felt like her body didn't belong to her anymore.

They were looking at her like she was something *other*. Not a person. A thing. A prize. A joke.

She was led to a stone platform near the pool. The Shadow Man gestured, and forced her on the cold slab. Her whole body shaking.

Then he spoke.

That voice. That *thing* he used as a voice. Deep and echoing, like it came from a whole other place, she never understood.

The words didn't make sense at first — not all of them but slowly she began to hear words

"...observe ..."
"...no need for help..."
"...record everything..."

They were talking about her.
Like she wasn't even there.

She bit the inside of her cheek so hard she tasted blood. she couldn't move, couldn't speak. Just stood there and felt *watched*.

She refused to look at the pool. Afraid that if she stared too long into that perfect stillness, it would show her something She didn't want to see, something she would never forget.

Her legs burned. Time dragged.

Minutes? Hours?

The crowd's silence stretched too long, like they were waiting for her to do something, break, or scream.

She almost did.

Almost screamed just to hear a human sound again.

Finally, the Shadow Man gave a small nod. As he approached her slowly, his footsteps were soundless even on the forest floor. She backed away instinctively, the fear already rising in her throat like bile. Her feet dragged against the moss and earth, but he reached her anyway — his arms cold and strong as they swept under her.

She screamed before she even understood what was happening.

"No! No, please—don't—"

He lifted her like she was nothing, like her weight didn't matter. She kicked. Hit his chest with her fists, struggled in his arms, but his grip didn't falter. He walked straight toward the pool with her clenched to him, ignoring her panic like it didn't exist.

The closer she got, the worse the air felt. Thicker. Colder. Her chest tightened with a pressure that wasn't just fear — it was something else, something deeper. She could hear the faintest humming in the air, like the water itself was alive and waiting.

The moment his foot touched the surface, ripples spread across the pool in smooth, unnatural circles. He didn't hesitate. He waded in slowly, the dark water rising higher up his legs, up to his waist — and then to her chest.

"No! Stop!" she gasped, choking on the edge of panic. " Please-please, don't!"

But he didn't stop.

He kept walking until the pool swallowed her whole.

The cold hit like knives. The water rushed over her face, into her ears, into her nose. She screamed but only bubbles escaped, racing to the surface above.

He dropped her under as her arms flailed. Her legs kicked. The pressure in her chest grew tighter and tighter until she thought it would tear her in half.

Then she saw them.

Shapes.

People.

They floated in the depths — half-formed figures, arms outstretched, faces pale and blurred by the dark. Some watched her. Some drifted like seaweed.

Her panic turned to terror as she clawed at his chest, nails digging in, mouth wide as she tried to scream again. Her vision flickered — flashes of blackness at the edges. Her chest buckled.

This is it, she thought. *He's going to let her drown.*

Her lungs gave out. Her body jerked, violently—

And then he pulled her up.

The surface shattered above her and she burst into the air with a ragged scream, choking and coughing, her throat burning, water gushing from her nose and mouth. She clung to him out of pure reflex as he held her just above the surface, her body limp and heaving.

He said nothing.

Just turned and carried her back through the trees.

He laid her down on the forest floor beneath a tangle of low branches, placing her gently on a patch of moss as if she were glass.

And then he stood over her, watching.

She couldn't meet his eyes. Curled in on herself, trying to understand what had just happened, trying not to sob too loud.

Why had he brought her up?
Why had he taken her down?

The crowd began talking again. Laughing. As if she'd just been part of some performance.

Two silent ones stepped forward and grabbed her arms as she was led back to the cabin. Bella followed like the good girl she was.

She collapsed onto her mattress.

Bella sat against the wall, arms wrapped around her legs, her head down.

Neither of them spoke.

What would they say?

That they were being watched? Measured? Tested for something they couldn't understand?

She curled into herself and pressed her face to the pillow, trying not to cry.

Trying not to think about the next time.

Because there *would* be a next time.

The Shadow Man didn't take them there for nothing.

And the pool was still out there. Waiting.

Chapter 17

Bella had been pacing the room for what felt like hours. Back and forth. Back and forth. Her eyes were glassy, her jaw tight.

She sat curled on the mattress, knees to her chest, doing what she always did — trying to disappear. Anything to ignore the storm brewing three steps away.

Then Bella stopped.

The sudden silence made her look up.

Bella was standing still in the middle of the room, eyes locked on me. Her face was twisted — not in pain, or sadness but red hot anger.

"This is your fault," Bella said, her voice low and shaking.

She blinked. "What?"

"You," Bella snapped, taking a step closer. "You *made* him angry. You kept looking at him. You always *look* at him."

Her heart started pounding. "Bella, I didn't—"

"You *want* him to notice you, don't you?" Bella hissed. "You think if you cry enough, if you look small enough, he'll protect you.

The words were so cruel, so wrong, they stole the breath from my lungs.

"I don't," she whispered. "Bella, stop. Please."

But Bella was already moving, pushing her hard.

She fell to the floor with a thud, Before she could move, Bella was on top of her — fists flying, screams turning into snarls.

"You always ruin everything! You ruin *everything!*"

She cried out, covering her face, curling up into a ball, but Bella scratched and shoved and hit, her whole body trembling with fury.

"Bella, please! Stop! *STOP!*"

The door slammed open.

And everything changed.

The Shadow Man entered like thunder, like a nightmare breaking through a dream. The room dropped ten degrees in an instant.

Bella froze. Her hand still raised, her chest heaving. She turned slowly, already knowing who was behind her.

His hand swung without warning. The sound of it — the *crack* — was louder than her scream. Bella's head snapped to the side as she collapsed onto the floor, scrambling away, crawling backwards, her hand pressed to her cheek. "I—I didn't mean—"

He didn't care.

Another slap.

Harder.

Bella whimpered, curling into herself. Her whole body shook. Her eyes — wide and broken and terrified.

The Shadow Man paused.

Then, slowly, his hand dropped to his side. He stared for a moment longer. His gaze wasn't angry. It wasn't anything. Just hollow.

Then he turned.

And walked out.

Bella stayed on the floor, curled up tight, her breath coming in sharp, hiccupping sobs.

She didn't look at me. Didn't reach out.

Just lay there — two broken girls in a box of wood and silence, whatever was there before — friendship, understanding, shared suffering — it had shattered.

There was no going back.

Chapter 18

The heavy scrape of the bedroom door jolted her heart into a gallop. She was on her feet by instinct—knees ready to bend, breath held like a rabbit caught in the open. She didn't struggle when they entered. She didn't scream. That would only make it worse.

But inside, a quiet dread uncoiled like smoke.

She glanced once at Bella, who sat still on the mattress, hugging her knees, eyes unreadable. Bella didn't speak. Didn't blink. Just stared as the faceless shadows seized her, one on each arm, and dragged her from the warmth of the stale room into the frost-laced dawn.

The fear clawed higher in her chest as they led her through the narrow hallway and into the woods. The air was colder out here, sharp and earthy, the kind that made your lungs burn. Mist hung low to the ground, curling around her bare feet like fingers trying to pull her under.

The trees swallowed her.

They brought her to a new clearing where the forest opened like a wound and machines rose from the dirt like bones.

Steel frames. Hanging bars. Pulleys. Chains.

All cold. All waiting.

She was shoved toward the first structure—an iron ladder leading skyward into the canopy.

A test.

No instructions. Just a gesture. Climb.

Her hands closed around the rung. Wet. Slippery. Her knuckles went white. Every muscle in her body screamed at her to turn back, to fall, to collapse and beg. But she climbed.

One rung. Then the next. Her arms burned. Her shoulder ached. She ignored it.

Higher.

A voice in her head—her own, but fiercer now—
pushed her, one more step. Don't fall. Please
don't give them the satisfaction.

She reached the top and waited, her chest rising
and falling, but they pointed again—a jump.

A rusted platform stretched a few feet away. Too
far. Too high. Too insane.

She hesitated.

If you fall, you break. If you hesitate, you fail.
And if you fail…you die.

She jumped.

Her feet slipped, but she landed. Pain flared in
her knee as it struck metal, but she was upright.

Another gesture. Another leap.

This one she missed.

The fall was short but brutal. Her body crumpled in the dirt. She couldn't breathe for a moment. Her ribs felt like cracked glass.

They gave her no time.

Before she could sit up, they dragged her again—to the next trial.

The bar.

A metal bar that was round in shape and spun in circles.

They made her grip it, as they pushed her off.

She spun faster and faster, until the breath left her body. She clung to the metal bar for dear life, digging in so she wouldn't be flung around like a ragdoll, the wind howling in her ears, the sky a blur.

She couldn't let go. Her grip was blood-slicked. Her arms stretched like pulled taffy. Her vision blackened at the edges.

Don't let go. Don't let go. Don't let go.

Her body betrayed her. Her fingers slipped as she crashed to the ground, broken.

Coughing. Heaving. The bile was bitter in her throat. Her head spun even as she lay on the ground.

She wanted to cry. To scream. But there was no time as they strapped her into a chair.

The chains groaning as they lifted her, suspending her above the forest floor like a puppet.

The chair began to swing.

Back and forth.
Back and forth.

Slow at first. Almost soothing.

Then higher. Wider.

It became a pendulum of pain. Her head knocked back and forth. Her stomach lurched. The trees spun again.

Then came the sickness.

Her body convulsed. She vomited down her front, choking and gasping. But the swinging didn't stop.

Tears ran sideways across her face as the wind screamed through her ears.

And in that moment, for the first time since she'd learned to stand, she broke.

Not her body—her will.

Her voice cracked as she screamed.

"Please—please! I'll go back! Just take me back to the cabin!"

The wind swallowed her words.

"I'll do anything—please!"

No answer.

Only the creak of metal and the clank of chain.

She sobbed, her arms limp, her throat raw. Her thoughts scattered, spinning with the trees.

I can't do this. I can't survive this. This isn't strength—it's cruelty. You're not training me. You're testing how much I can bear before I break.

She felt herself slipping.

Into despair. Into numbness.

Then, just as suddenly as it began, the chains slowed. The spinning eased. The chair was lowered.

They unbuckled her. Dropped her into the dirt.

She didn't move.

She barely breathed.

But in the blur of nausea and pain, she heard something.

Steps. Heavy. Deliberate.

The Shadow Man.

He stood over her. Watching.

And she, broken and shivering, whispered into the mud:

"Please. I want the cage. I'll go back. Just take me home."

Even her defeat sounded like a vow.

Chapter 19

The tension between her and Bella had finally begun to thaw.

Their every word had been laced with guarded suspicion for days, maybe weeks. Two prisoners circling each other like strays—neither willing to trust, both too bruised by the world outside their room. But now the silence between them had changed its shape. It had stopped biting. It breathed.

They talked in low voices, sitting shoulder to shoulder on the edge of their mattresses, never quite looking each other in the eye.

Bella had snorted at something she said about how the Shadow Man tilted his head like a curious crow.

"You're not supposed to laugh in here," Bella muttered, her lips twitching.

That was last night.

This morning, everything changed.

The door opened early. Too early. The metal
screamed on its hinges, and she sat up with a
jolt, heart in her throat. The handlers stepped
in, faceless as ever, their movements measured
and cold. She flinched, expecting them to come
for her.

But they didn't.

They looked past her.

Straight at Bella.

Bella stood slowly. Not frightened—resigned.
She didn't say a word. Didn't even look at her
until she was halfway to the door. Then, just
before stepping out, she turned her head
slightly.

Their eyes met.

Bella's gaze was unreadable—flat, but not
uncaring. A flicker of something lived there: a
warning. Or maybe... an apology.

The door shut behind her with a dull finality.

And she was alone.

At first, she didn't move. Just stared at the door, expecting it to open again. For Bella to be shoved back in, groaning and bruised, complaining under her breath. That's how it went, didn't it? She always came back.

Except... the hours passed.

The light from the hallway dimmed and brightened again, the faint shift of artificial day and night filtered through the cracks in the walls.

And still no Bella.

She paced. Sat. Paced again. Her hands fidgeted. Her eyes kept drifting to the empty mattress, as if Bella might appear there if she looked hard enough. But it stayed untouched, a hollow echo of where someone used to be.

The silence pressed in.

The room felt wrong without her. Too still. Too quiet. The shadows stretched longer than usual, creeping across the floor like something alive.

She tried to distract herself—she sorted the blanket, stacked the cup, and ran her fingers over the old carvings in the wall. "HELP" was scratched in jagged letters beneath the mattress. She hadn't noticed it before.

The quiet stretched into agony.

And then, just as the light began to fade again into evening, a scream.

It came from beyond the door. High. Ragged. Human.

She froze.

Then—another scream. Louder. Shattering.

Her chest tightened.

"Bella?" she whispered.

More screaming. Choking sobs.

It was her.

"Bella!" she shouted, scrambling to the door. "I'm here! I'm here!"

She pounded on the door with both fists. "Let me out—let me out, she needs help!"

Nothing.

Only more crying. Guttural, broken. Not just pain—but fear.

The kind that tore at your soul.

She pressed her ear to the door, listening, quietly sobbing. She could hear Bella gasping, pleading—then something she couldn't make out. Then a hard, violent sound. A thud.

A final scream.

Then—silence.

That horrible, living silence.

The kind that fills your lungs with dread and tells you not to breathe too loudly.

She sank to the floor, hands trembling, forehead against the door. She whispered Bella's name again and again like a mantra, but the sound cracked and vanished into the air.

No answer.

No echo.

Just her own breath, shallow and fast, and the ringing in her ears.

She crawled back to the mattress but didn't lie down. She sat, arms around her knees, rocking slightly. Her thoughts spun like a broken wheel.

What had they done to her? Why didn't they bring her back? Would she come back at all?

The room felt unbearable without Bella's presence to balance it. She missed her sharp tongue, her grim wisdom, her muttered warnings. Even the silences they shared had been shared with another person.

Now, everything was hers alone.

And she hated it.

The mattress across the room remained empty, like a question no one would answer.

She stared at it until her eyes blurred.

In that moment, despair wrapped around her like a second skin.

Not because she was alone.

But because she now knew how much she needed someone else.

Hope flickered. Faint. Weak. But still there.

She clung to it with shaking hands.

Because if she let go—if Bella didn't return—

Then she wasn't sure who she would become in the dark.

Chapter 20

She couldn't breathe.

Her chest was tight, her ribs pressing against her lungs as she lay in the cage again, her arms wrapped around herself, her fingers digging into the fabric of her gown.

The room felt too small.

The walls too close.

Her skin too tight.

Every breath she took felt like it wasn't enough—like the air in the room was thinning, suffocating her in slow, agonising increments.

She needed out. She needed space.

She needed to do something.

Her vision blurred as she pushed herself up, her arms trembling beneath her own weight.

Her hands moved without thinking.

She grabbed the wooden stool in the corner and threw it, her breath coming in short, sharp bursts as it crashed against the wall.

The ceramic bowl on the floor—smashed, shards scattering in all directions, water seeping into the cracks of the wooden floor.

Her nails clawed at the thin mattress, ripping into the fabric, pulling out stuffing, making it useless.

She was breathing too fast now.

Her body was moving on instinct—desperate, frenzied, wild.

The blankets—kicked into the corner. The floor—scratched raw beneath her nails.

She didn't stop. She couldn't stop.

Her body had to do something, had to move, had to destroy, had to do something.

The door slammed open.

She barely had time to turn before he was on her.

Hands—grabbing, yanking.

A sharp slap to her face.

The impact sent a white-hot shock through her entire body, her breath stolen, her knees buckling as she collapsed to the floor.

Her forehead hit the floor.

Her vision flickered, her pulse slamming against her temples, her mind spiralling into a dull, ringing void of pain and breathlessness.

She gasped for air—but there was none.

Her ribs wouldn't expand, her stomach felt empty and pained, her limbs weak and unresponsive.

A hand fisted into her hair.

Her head snapped back, her throat stretching painfully as she was forced to look up—

At him.

At the shadow man.

Watching.

Always bloody watching.

Then, He backhanded her across her face.

Her head whipped sideways, the iron taste of blood blooming in her mouth as her lip split open. another smack and flash of pain as blood sprayed on the floor.

She barely had time to register it before—

A hand to her ass.

Sudden. Hard. Sharp.

Something cracked.

She crumpled sideways, her body folding into itself, her hands barely catching her fall as she gasped—a strangled, pitiful sound.

The world tilted.

Her vision blurred.

Her heartbeat roared in her ears.

She couldn't think anymore.

There was only pain.

Only the weight of all of him.

A second smack.

Then a third, it felt like more people had joined in.

She tried to curl up—to protect herself, but there was nowhere to go.

No way to hide from the violence pressing down on her like a storm.

A hand pressed into her back.

Her chest hit the floor.

She wheezed, her ribs flaring in protest, her lungs struggling to expand beneath the pressure.

She wasn't breathing right.

Her heartbeat wasn't right.

Nothing was right.

A hand ghosted over her jaw, smearing blood across her lips, into her hair.

She flinched, but she couldn't move away.

The shadow man crouched beside her.

Spoke. His voice was calm, measured, like nothing had happened.

Like she wasn't on the floor, battered and bruised, her skin burning, her bones aching beneath the force of every hit.

She didn't need to understand him.

She knew what he was saying.

You will not fight.

You will not resist.

You are nothing.

You belong to me.

Her breath hitched.

A sound crawled up her throat—not a sob, not a scream, just a hollow, broken sound trying desperately to escape.

The pressure lifted.

The boots stepped back.

The shadow man left.

The door shut.

She didn't move for a long time.

Her cheek was pressed against the floor, the cool wood a contrast to the heat of her burning skin.

Her ribs ached.

Her lip throbbed.

Her body was a wreck of pain and exhaustion.

But worse than that, her mind was empty.

She had felt rage before. She had felt fear. She had felt helpless. But this?

This was something else.

Something worse.

Something final.

The room was destroyed, and so was she.

She had thought she could fight back.

That some part of her still had control.

That she still mattered.

But they had proved her wrong.

She was nothing.

She was a body to be moved.

A thing to be punished.

A thing to be owned, used and abused.

She squeezed her eyes shut, swallowing the taste of blood and defeat.

She wanted to disappear.

To become so small that she ceased to exist.

And maybe—maybe she already had.

Chapter 21

Days melted into one another, each identical to the last.

Wake. Clean. Walk. Sleep.

Again. Again. Again.

She was no longer a person; she was just something to be used and controlled.

She had stopped wondering if this was a nightmare.

Nightmares ended. This didn't.

She worked from the moment she was woken— hauled from sleep, shoved into movement before her body was ready.

No words. No kindness. Just expectation.

She scrubbed the floors until her hands bled. Then, she carried buckets of water from the pump outside, the metal handles digging into her palms, her arms trembling under the weight.

She cleaned the dishes, her fingers submerged in cold, murky water, the sharp scent of blood filling her nose.

She swept the dusty wooden floors, coughing as it filled her lungs, her body aching with exhaustion.

Every task felt impossible. But she had no choice.

The beatings were frequent now.

She didn't need to fight back to be punished; the memories were always there.

Sometimes, they hit her to remind her she was worse than nothing, and other times, they hit her because she simply *was* nothing.

She learned to move faster, stay silent, and keep her head down.

It didn't stop the pain she felt.

But it helped.

They still paraded her through the woods, the rope always tight against her chest and shoulders,

The first few times, she had thought—maybe this is my chance.

But there was never a chance.

He was always watching.

Always waiting for her to resist, to fight, to try to run.

She had tried once—just a flicker of hesitation, a half-step backward.

The response had been immediate.

The rope had yanked tight; She had stumbled, coughing, gasping for air, her lungs burning.

And he laughed.

He dragged her forward like a disobedient dog, the rope cutting into her shoulders, the bruise lingering for days.

She never tried again. Now, she walks when he tells her to.

She stood when he told her to stand.

She let the people in the clearing touch her, inspect her, measure her. Grab for her.

There was nothing left to fight for.

It always came during the walks.

Before they put her on display, they ensured she was clean, like it mattered and needed to be presentable. The same hands, stripping her. The same rough scrubbing, the cloth scraping her raw.

She stopped shivering.

She stopped resisting.

She stopped feeling.

The shadow man was always there.

Watching.

His gaze on her skin was worse than the scrubbing, cold water, and bruises.

He wasn't just examining her wounds. He was making sure she knew he gave them to her.

She belonged to him.

She would always belong to him.

Yet still, she was made to sleep beside Bella. But it wasn't the same. Bella hated her.

She saw it in the way she turned her back on her every night.

The way she shoved her aside when they were forced to share a blanket.

The way she glared, her dark eyes sharp and unforgiving.

The first night after a terrible beating, she had whispered, voice hoarse, barely more than a breath—

"Why do you hate me?"

Bella had been still for a long moment.

Then—a bitter laugh. Not cruel. Just tired.

She turned her head slightly, her face shadowed in the dim light.

Then, in their language, she spat a single word.

"Weak."

It cut deeper than the bruises. She curled into a ball, pressing her face against the mattress, feeling her ribs ache with every breath.

Bella was right. She was weak. She had let them break her.

She had let them win.

And she didn't know how to fix it.

Whenever new strangers arrived, they paraded her out.

It didn't matter if she had just finished a chore.

It didn't matter if she was bleeding, limping, shaking from the last beating.

She was paraded.

She never fought. Why bother? It had never helped in the past.

It only made everything worse.

She stood when he told her to stand.

She let them touch her, let their fingers press into her arms, trace her jaw, pull on her hair.

The people always chatted, discussing her; she was a disgusting thing, no better than merchandise.

She never looked anyone in the eyes. Not anymore.

That had been beaten out of her a long time ago.

She used to think that one day, someone would find her—some hero who would fall madly in love with her, whisk her away, and give her the happy ever after she was meant to have. Alas, no one came; no one even looked her way. She was just a sad, pathetic excuse for a human.

There would be no road to recovery, no house, no voice to soothe her soul.

She had seen the woods. There was nothing out there. There was no one looking for her.

The world had moved on.

She was a forgotten thing, lost in the shadows of people who only saw her as a body.

One day, she knew something worse would come.

Something final.

Something she wouldn't walk away from.

She didn't know when, where or how.

But she felt it deep in her bones, almost prayed for it.

She had to do something. She had to escape.

But how do you escape when you no longer care or remember what freedom feels like?

Chapter 22

She woke choking on her breath.

Something had her by the ankle—*dragging* her across the mattress. Cold, not the cold you feel through your skin, but the kind that sinks into your bones and whispers to your nerves that something is wrong.

He stood at the foot of her bed.

The Shadow Man.

A silhouette made of nightmares. No face. No voice. Just a shape so black it swallowed the light. Limbs long and warped, moving like smoke wrapped around sinew. He was impossible to see fully and somehow even harder to unsee.

She screamed.

His hand whipped out—five gnarled fingers like twisted wood—and seized my face. Skin against the skin if that was skin. It felt like frostbite, wet and dead and biting all at once. Her scream turned to a muffled, breathless whine. He pulled her off the bed with a crack of spine against the frame, and she slammed to the floor like a carcass. This time, she was dragging her by the hair—down a hallway that hadn't been there the night before.

The bathroom. Her bathroom, but not. The tiles were blackened and rotted. The mirror was shattered. The light flickered and buzzed with flies.

The tub was full.

Of water?

No. Of something thicker. Grey. Filmy. The stench of rot and bleach hit her so hard she gagged.

He dropped her in.

The liquid stung like acid. She thrashed, screamed, and tried to climb out—but he forced her back down, one palm pressing on her sternum. She couldn't move. Could barely breathe. Then he produced a brush.

It wasn't just coarse—it was *cruel*.

Bristles stiff with dried filth. spiked wires poking out like teeth. He began scrubbing—starting with her chest, scraping over her breasts until the skin turned red, then raw, then bleeding. He didn't stop. He moved down to her stomach, her thighs, the backs of her knees. Every stroke tore something away. Dirt. Or pieces of *her*.

She screamed until her throat went dry.

When he reached her scalp, he dug the brush into her hair like he wanted to peel it from her skull. Clumps of hair floated in the water, matted with soap and blood. Her body was shivering violently, half-numb, half on fire. Her skin felt new, stripped raw like a skinned rabbit.

When he stopped, she prayed he would leave.

But he didn't.

She tried to back away, slipping into the mess of water and blood.

"No…" she whispered. "Please…"

He pulled her to her feet.

She could barely stand. Her legs were trembling sticks beneath her. But he didn't care. He yanked her arm, and she stumbled forward, trailing a path of blood and bathwater behind her. Her wrists were free, but her hands were too numb to fight. She followed, half-dragged, out of the bathroom.

Chapter 23

She didn't struggle when they came for her again. She had learned that fighting back only made it worse.

Her body moved where they forced it to, her feet stumbling on the floor as they dragged her through the cabin. The hand around her wrist was tight, the pressure biting into her skin.

Something felt different today.

The house was too alive, filled with noise, voices murmuring, an energy that felt wrong.

She didn't understand.

She didn't want to understand.

Then—

The doors opened. And the noise hit her like a heat wave.

It was full of people. More than she had ever seen gathered in one place before.

Men. Women. Children.

They filled the room, standing along the walls, crowding the edges of the space, their voices low, expectant.

A fire burned in the hearth, flickering against wooden walls, casting long, shifting shadows.

And at the centre

A chair, so high off the ground, he forced her into it and pulled the ropes tight, securing her shoulders to the wooden frame, the strap around her stomach digging in painfully.

Tighter than necessary.

Like they were preparing her for something.

Her breath came fast, chest rising and falling in quick, uneven movements.

This wasn't normal. This wasn't like before.

The room fell silent.

And then,

He entered—the man.
The firelight stretched his frame as he moved,
slow, deliberate, his steps measured.

He wasn't looking at her.

But she felt him.

Always watching.

Something shifted in the air as he approached.

The others reacted to him, eyes gleaming with
something she didn't understand.

Then

The cheering began.

Loud. Sudden. Deafening.

Laughter broke through the room, rolling over
her like a suffocating wave.

She flinched, shaking, her mind scrambling to make sense of it.

The man stepped closer. As she shrank back, there was nowhere to escape to, where could she go.

The crowd cheered for him. Laughing at her.

Like they were celebrating.

Then a flash from a stranger who jumped in front of her taking her picture, people gathering around to see.

Why wouldn't they want photos of her tied to a chair, of course, they had to remember this in full detail.

A plate was placed in front of her.

A cake.

Small. Round. Covered in thick, white icing.

At first, it was nothing.

Just food.

Something she hadn't had in so long. Her stomach twisted in hunger, but something felt off.

Then she saw it.

The words.

Written in red icing, neat and deliberate.

HAPPY 3rd BIRTHDAY.

Her breath stopped.

Her pulse pounded against her ribs, against her throat, against her skull.

Her vision blurred, her mind folding in on itself. The words blurred together.

HAPPY 3rd BIRTHDAY.

No.

That wasn't right.

That wasn't possible.

Her body locked up, muscles tightening, breath caught in her chest.

She didn't—

She hadn't—

She had been trapped here longer than that.

Hadn't she?

The laughter grew louder.

A woman tilted her chin up, forcing her to look at the cake and see it.

She tried to pull away, but the ropes held her still.

They were still cheering.

Still laughing.

Like this was funny.

Like this was normal.

Her mind screamed, trying to push through the fog, trying to grasp at memories, trying to make sense of the wrongness sinking into her skin.

She had been held here for months or years. Hadn't she? Or had it been longer? Had it been forever?

Had she even been anywhere else?

Time must be broken.

This. This mockery. This lie.

The shadow man stood beside her now. Close enough that she could feel him. Feel his presence pressing against her, crushing her.

She could sense his gaze on her skin.

Measuring. Calculating. Satisfied.

He leaned in, his breath warm against her ear.

She flinched, every part of her screaming to run, fight, or do something.

But she was tied down to this chair, with nowhere to go.

He leaned in to show her the photo.

That couldn't be right; it showed a toddler. She wasn't a toddler, was she?

She was a woman.

The photo was in front of her, evidence, proof.

The shadow man spoke—a soft, low murmur in his language.

She understood the words. But when had that happened?

"Happy Birthday, beautiful girl."

The room erupted in cheers again. The sound
filled her ears, her cake sat untouched before
her as the world glitched in her mind,
everything breaking apart right in front of her—

She had always believed she was a prisoner.

The bars that stretched high above her head
were the first things she remembered. Cold.
Unclimbable. They boxed her in, kept her small
and helpless. She screamed, sometimes for
hours, and no one came. In her mind, the cot
became a cage. A wooden fortress she could
never escape.

But she was only a baby then.

She didn't have the words for "safe" or
"protection." Only feelings—loud,
overwhelming, confusing feelings that painted
the world with fear. In her eyes, shaped by
shadows, cries, and moments she couldn't
name, everything became something it wasn't.

She saw a man, always standing in the doorway.

Tall. Silent. His face hidden in the dim light of the hallway. To her, he became something terrifying—the Shadow Man. He never spoke, not because he didn't care, but because she couldn't yet understand the gentle hush of his voice, the tired kindness in his silence. He moved slowly, carefully, always just beyond her reach. And that made him a monster in her mind.

She thought he came to hurt her.

When he lifted her from the cot—crying, writhing—she believed she was being taken. When he held her over the warm bathwater and wiped her skin clean, she thought she was being punished. The roughness of the towel, the water in her eyes, the sting of soap—all of it blurred into something cruel.

But the truth was much softer.

He was just bathing her, changing her, and cradling her head when it lolled against his chest. He was the one who stayed up when she was sick, who sang wordless lullabies she forgot

by morning. The Shadow Man was never a
threat. He was a father.

The bottles of milk weren't a way to starve her,
but the only nourishment her body could
handle.

The endless walks outside tied around her
shoulders were simply him teaching her to walk.
The lake where she almost drowned, he was
teaching her to swim like fathers do. Why did
she imagine the worst every time?

She remembered the woods too—dark shapes,
metal groans, and sudden bursts of shrieking.
She thought she was being taken to a place full
of machines. Dangerous. Loud. But as she grew,
the sounds came into focus. The screeching was
laughter. The machines were swings. The
monsters were children, shouting with joy as
they played.

Even the girl, Bella.

The one she thought was her rival—the one who grabbed her toys and pushed her on the floor.

For so long, she believed that girl was part of the nightmare—another captor, another shadow in the story. But they were just two small girls struggling to share space, love, and attention. Just two sisters doing what siblings do—fighting, yelling, needing attention.

As her memories took shape, so did the truth.

There was no cage.
There was no monster.
There was no kidnapping.

Now, she saw it all for what it was.

Not horror.

Just childhood.

www.ingramcontent.com/pod-product-compliance
Lightning Source LLC
Chambersburg PA
CBHW060935030726
47503CB00003B/604